KING OF SINNERS

LORDS OF LAS VEGAS

TAMMY ANDRESEN

SWIFT ROMANCE PUBLISHING CORP

❀ Created with Vellum

KING OF SINNERS

A deal with a cold billionaire...a desperate coed who has run out of options...

Ruthless
  Lethal
  Handsome as sin
  The devil has always been wrapped in a tempting package.

And that's Mason Kincaid. King of Vegas and of sinners. He owns half this town and runs the other half with an iron fist.

He's pretty much everything I've learned to avoid. I dated his brother a few years back when I thought a bad boy would be fun. It did not take long for me to learn the Kincaids are not fun. They are *the* snakes in the garden...

Now, I'm on the straight and narrow. Work. Class. Repeat. Head down...no bad boys in sight. I'm just trying to get my degree so I can escape Vegas and the Kincaids.

Until one night when I took a shortcut home after a late shift. Now, I'm a witness to a crime with a price on my head.

There is only one man I can turn to for protection and that's Mason Kincaid. King of Vegas…

But the price?

The King of Vegas, he charges more than most.

What he wants…

My virginity.

Welcome to the Dark side of Las Vegas where the stakes are even higher and the men more lethal… *King of Sinners* if the first book in the "Lords of Las Vegas" series, but don't worry… there will be more! Coming soon…

King of Sinners
King of Temptation
King of Wrath
King of Pain
King of Ruin

NOTE TO READERS

Dear Readers,

First, thank you so much for choosing to read *King of Sinners*. I've been moving toward writing this series for a very long time.

For anyone who doesn't know me, I started my career in Regency romance. My best-selling series, *Lords of Scandal*, is about the English elite who run an illegal gaming hell, the historical word for casino, the Den of Sins.

In the words of Guy Ritchie's, *The Gentleman*, the British Elite were the world's original gangsters. My bestie in life and in the writing world, Maggie Dallen, read one of them about six years ago and said, "Tammy, you should take the Lords of Scandal descendants to Vegas."

But let me tell you, the idea of it was scary! Then, a year later, another writing friend said the same thing. And then a reader, and then another. And so on, until I couldn't ignore it anymore. Yeah...the Brits were going to invade the States. Oh wait, that happened already!

And just to be clear, "Lords of Las Vegas" needed its own beginning, so it does not start with a British family, but with an American one. Though, spoiler alert, you don't have to look hard to see where the British players will enter the scene.

But be warned, these are even darker, even steamier than my historicals. For my fans, read on only if that interests you.

For my friends and family…thank you for buying. Your support means so much! Now, please close this book and never open it again. We do not want to make eye contact in Walmart, or over the Thanksgiving table, after you've read this book.

And now I'll stop blathering and let you get started on *King of Sinners*! For anyone new, I am so excited to share the beginning of what I hope to be a long and deliciously dirty series about the Lords of Las Vegas.

All my best,

Tammy

STALK ME LIKE AN ALPHA!

Join my newsletter to get all the latest updates!

Tammy's Newsletter

And follow me everywhere else for teasers, giveaway, book news and fun!

www.authortammyandresen.com
www.facebook.com/authortammyandresen
www.instagram.com/tammyandresen
https://www.tiktok.com/@lordsoflasvegas
www://amazon.com/authortammyandresen

PROLOGUE

The hum of really good champagne and the thumping of techno music pulse through me as a hand circles my waist. My date…Leo Kincaid.

Leo is the sort of rich that could make a girl conveniently forget all her principles, coupled with his good looks, I didn't hesitate when he asked me out. Now, it's our third date and his hands have been all over me tonight.

We're at one of the clubs his family owns. The lights flash, spinning in way that makes my head spin too. I sway a bit and Leo pulls me close, his body pressing to mine. I can't help it, I stiffen away.

I'm no good at this. I hate conflict, it's never been my thing. And, in my defense, I have no dating experience to fall back on. Which means tonight is a double whammy of *I don't know what to do.*

I'm not so naïve, that I don't get what he wants. I'm just not sure how to tell him that I don't think I'm giving it to him. I've never been with any man before, I'm a virgin, and this is moving so fast.

Maybe it's because I'm older. Twenty and dating men, not boys.

But also, rich and handsome does not equal patient. Even I know that.

I came from a nowhere Nebraska town that is filled with nothing but cornfields, I swear, and moving to Las Vegas to attend UNLV has been an adjustment. It was easy to resist the farm boys. Even with all their muscles, they were just that…boys. And I wasn't too tempted by the frat boys either. They were everywhere and seemed all the same to me. Besides, I had a scholarship to keep.

And my dad, he got my mom pregnant when they were both really young. My mom left and my dad raised me on his own. He made me promise not to give myself to someone until I was ready. Until it felt right.

When he died, that was like a mantra. Save myself for the right guy…

So I've put off having sex because I hadn't met the one. And at some point, it became easier not to date at all then to try and explain.

But Leo Kincaid came into the bar that I work at, Rebel's, and he had that swagger. More man than I've ever seen. When he asked me out, I said yes. And I felt pretty good about it. All my friends had had sex. It was time. Wasn't it? I felt pretty sure about the decision.

That was until I met his brother…

Last night we went to Leo's family home for dinner. I was surprised that's where he was taking me for a second date. But he told me that after his dad's death, he and his brothers were super tight. One more thing we had in common, no parents.

I was excited to meet his brothers, and introducing me to the family felt like a sign that he was kind of serious about me too.

All three Kincaid brothers were there. They have a sister too, but she's away at school.

I met Leo's youngest brother first. Roman Kincaid is a few years older than me, practically a frat boy himself. Not interesting at all.

And then Leo spun me around to his older brother and the head of the Kincaid family. Mason Kincaid.

Mason is a king. I don't know how I know this, I just do. It's in every line of his powerful body, the cut of his jaw, the glint in his eye. I kept my eyes down all dinner, barely speaking to keep from staring, and to keep Leo from noticing. I was completely and instantly in lust with his brother. All the while Leo's hand was climbing up my thigh. Awkward, I know...

Only Mason could outshine Leo, but I can't continue to date Leo when the attraction to his brother pulses though me like some kind of brand.

Now we're on our third date and three glasses of champagne in, I'm trying to work up the nerve to tell Leo that this isn't going happen. He doesn't strike me as the sort of man who's used to hearing the word *no*.

I drain my glass and push away from his hard chest. The club has some random name I can't remember, which isn't like me at all. I think it might be Temptation, but I can't say for certain. I know the Kincaids own it, like half of these kind of places on the strip. Usually, details are my thing. But tonight, I'm nervous and I can't seem to keep anything in my head.

Leo catches my arm and pulls me back into his embrace. "Come on, babe."

And then his hand snakes around my waist, crushing my belly to his.

"Leo," I start, trying to infuse my voice with some sort of authority. Disapproval at least.

"We're having a good time," he says, sliding his hand over my ass.

"No," I say, looking away. Because I'm not and the alcohol isn't making this any easier. I thought I could loosen up, let go. The few guys I've dated all ended up calling me a prude, and maybe I am. But I've just never really wanted them. But you can't tell a guy like Leo, *Sorry, you're just not doing it for me*.

Because that's the thing about being really into details. I notice them all. Dirt under the fingernails, weak set to the jaw, twitches that betray confidence as false. An awkward walk, a nervous twitch... And once I see these little things that betray confidence as false, I can't unsee them.

And that's when I catch a set of eyes across the room. Mason. Our gazes lock, my lips parting in a gasp.

My body starts to hum in a way I've never felt before, like tendrils of electricity sparking all through me.

Casually leaning against the bar, he still conveys the sort of power that has my mouth going dry as my gaze moves down the long, hard length of him and then back up to his eyes.

And then he's off the bar and moving toward us, our gazes still locked. I can barely breathe as he stalks closer.

His body has the natural sway of a lion crossing the savannah, or some other supreme predator that I can't think of because my brain has ceased working. An ache starts between my legs.

Leo's hand grasps my elbow, his body moving close to mine, as his lips come to my ear. "We should get out of here."

I don't answer, unable to look away, unable to form words. He gives my elbow a tug, causing me to lose my balance in the heels I'm wearing. My dress is knee length, I was going for less available with the length, but it keeps me from being able to widen my stance and I'm falling before I can correct.

Another hand grabs my waist and just like that, I'm straight again. I'm tall for a woman but I'm craning my neck, my chin lifting as I meet Mason's gaze again.

He's even better up close. The jaw, the cheekbones, the slash of his brows and the perfect tousled wave of his dark hair.

There is a slight crook in his nose, but it doesn't come off as a flaw. No, it only makes him look more masculine.

His hand is still at my waist as he quirks a single brow. "Shorter heels next time?"

I know it's not the heels but the alcohol, but I only give a nod. "Thank you," I murmur, licking my lips in my nervousness.

"My pleasure," he answers, his eyes locked on my tongue. I quickly pull it back in my mouth, heat climbing up my throat.

"What do you want, Mason?" Leo sounds pissed. Can't say I blame him. I haven't been able to tear my eyes away from his brother. It's the reason I need to find some strength and end this date.

"I want you to take Charlotte and go."

"Where?"

"Anywhere," Mason answers, an ominous note creeping into his voice. "Just not here."

"Why?"

But Mason doesn't get a chance to answer. From behind us the lights flicker and then a blast like a gunshot fills the air.

In a second, I'm crushed to Mason's chest, my body wrapped in his powerful arms. A scream escapes my lips as I burrow into him.

"Close your eyes," Mason whispers in my ear. Or is he yelling? The noise around is deafening. "And don't open them."

I do as he commands, not asking why in this moment, just glad for the protection of his large, powerful frame.

"What the fuck was that?" Leo bellows at his brother.

"Trouble," Mason answers. "Keep those eyes closed, Charlotte." And then I'm being lifted into his arms. He's warm and solid and so strong, he's like a port in a storm and I absolutely curl into him.

But the comfort of his body doesn't last long. "Take her," he says to Leo, "Go to my limo and wait for me there."

"What are you going to do?" Leo asks, taking me from his brother's arms.

"I'm going to clean up this mess," Mason answers. "And Charlotte, don't forget to keep those eyes closed. You're far too beautiful to be one more detail we have to clean up."

My blood runs cold as Leo carries me out of the club.

CHAPTER ONE

CHARLOTTE

"I CAN'T."

These are not words I usually say to my boss, but the guy has asked me to stay late every night this week and I've got the biggest project of my life due at the end of this week. I've got to ace this one, graduate, and finally leave Vegas.

The glittering city of lights has a dark side and I'm tired of being under its heel. Well, it's not Vegas's heel, really, it's the Kincaids's.

I shiver as I remember that night. The one where I realized that I was dating a monster, and his brother, the one I was ridiculously attracted to, was the biggest bad guy of them all.

I push a section of my long brown hair back from my face. I'm the only brunette on staff. At least, I'm the only one that's still a brunette. I've been working here for years and despite not looking like a typical Vegas girl, I make the kind of tips that has paid my rent and the gap in tuition my scholarship doesn't cover.

"Sorry, Char, but Candy and Destiny called in sick. I'm stuck." We all have silly names in this place, it helps to keep the customers from tracking us down outside of work. Something I should have remembered two years ago when I told Leo my full name.

Gus scratches at his neck, sweat making the back of his hair wet. He's got to be pushing fifty and he's got the extra weight around the middle to show for it.

Not that I dislike Gus. He keeps it professional and he keeps his temper. Both characteristics I really appreciate in a man with power over me.

"Look, Gus, I know I usually take the shifts, but I've got to work on the editing for my project and I could use a few more pictures too. All those extra tips won't mean anything if I have to pay for another semester." My scholarship ends at the finish of this term, my four years up, and if I don't pass my visual arts class, I'm doomed.

It's the class that should be an easy A for me, but my professor has been giving me a really hard time. He's Kincaid-worthy.

Actually, he's worse. The Kincaids only threatened my life. My professor? He's trying to blackmail me into having sex with him. Creep.

I need to get out of this city. Every day I stay is a day closer to the Kincaids deciding I'm a problem they don't feel like keeping around.

Maybe they've forgotten about me? It's possible. Except, sometimes, I can't shake the feeling I'm being watched. Maybe I've just grown incredibly paranoid, but either way, a change of scenery would do me good.

"I'll give you tomorrow night off if you'll stay tonight." Gus holds his thick hands up in a plea. "I know I can count on you, Char. I'm not trying to screw you over."

I let out a long breath, looking down at Gus. At five feet eight inches, I'm taller than him by a few inches normally, but he also insists the waitresses wear these ridiculous platforms as part of our uniform, so I tower over him now.

Tugging at my super-short skirt, I sigh. "Fine. I'll stay."

But inwardly, I cringe. I have this project planned that's going to force Professor Burke to pass me. Leaning into my strength, photography, it's a piece on the gritty beauty of Vegas. The small things that actually make this place beautiful but usually go unseen.

But I need time to get those shots, and finish all the edits, and I've had so little of that lately.

With a sigh, I tie my apron back on, and adjust my skintight white top that's part of our uniform. My boobs have always been bigger than anything else on me, which makes the shirt strain across them. It's a detail I dislike but I ignore it, just like I do most details in this place.

Or I try…

Moving to the next table, I start taking orders and bringing drinks, the night passing in a blur of alcohol, not that I'm drinking.

I've mostly steered clear, other than an occasional glass of wine with dinner. By two in the morning, when we finally close, I'm exhausted and wondering if I ought to change my stance and have a shot of vodka.

I don't even know how I'm going to drag myself home tonight.

Taking off my platforms, I pull on decent walking shoes, white sneakers, to make the trip faster. Then, I collect up my money and start for my shit apartment. Rebel's is on the edge of new Las Vegas.

But my place…it's in the dumps. A tiny studio, at least I get to live alone. I've always liked things to be orderly, neat. But after my dad died, my former roommates said I became obsessive. Whether I'm difficult or they're pigs, it's much easier to live alone.

I usually stay on the main drag to get home, but it takes longer and I'm just too tired tonight. So cutting down first one alley and then another, I work my way east, eager for the sanctuary of my bed.

I just want to sleep and then I'll worry about life tomorrow. At least my apron pocket is full of tips. Money I can add to my collection for when I leave this place.

My plan is to go to New York with my best friend, Kim. I know that city has just as many sharks as this place, but first, I won't have accidentally dated one of them and second, I need to be in a hub of some kind.

My major is marketing, but my passion is photography. Two

things that pair rather nicely but only if I can get a job at a marketing firm with a department big enough to create some of its own marketing materials.

I tug at my skirt, which has ridden up at the quick clip I'm currently walking and take the final corner before I reach my street.

Where I stop dead in my tracks.

Fifty feet down the dark alley are three men, one on his knees, one holding him, and the third pointing a gun at his head.

I squeeze my eyes shut, sure that I'm imagining this whole thing, but there is just enough light from the flickering streetlamp at the end of the block to cast the scene in shadowy light.

I can't see anyone's faces, but I can see enough to know what's happening and my blood runs cold with fear.

And then the gun pops off, making me startle. I don't mean to, but a small cry falls from my lips as my hands raise to my mouth to cover it.

But it's too late. Both men still standing look at me. The one not holding a gun barely hesitates for a second before he starts charging straight for me.

I scream again, not trying to hold it in as I spin, the treads of my sneakers helping me to pick up speed as I break into a run, my longer legs, stretching out to move as quickly as possible.

But it isn't fast enough. I can hear him gaining and my lungs strain as another scream builds in my chest.

He's going to catch me. Will he kill me? Worse?

I'm losing energy, my legs turning to jelly and my body slowing as a broken sob breaks from my lips. Where am I even going?

The high rev on an engine stops me in my tracks as a car appears from the street on my left. The sleek black sedan stops in front of me, the tires screeching, as the driver's door whips open and a man steps out.

He's got the car between him and me but our eyes lock as he pulls out a gun. A giant gun.

A gun like I've never seen before. I think I've gone numb. This should send me to the ground with fear, but I don't feel a thing. Is he going to shoot me? Dimly, a list of things I wish I'd done flashes through my mind.

I wish I'd visited my dad's grave more. I wish I'd graduated college. Would have made him proud. I wish I'd had mind-blowing sex...

"Stop," he snarls.

"I am," I whisper my hands going up.

But his eyes are not on me, they're behind me, and that's when I realize he's not speaking to me at all.

I turn my head to see both men who'd been chasing me also stopped, ten feet behind me with their hands in the air.

"Get in, princess."

I know he's talking to me. My brain won't even start on whether or not I think it's a good idea to get in the car with the man who's holding a giant weapon. I can't get my legs to work. "I..."

"Get. In. Now."

Something about his tone, the command, I obey, stuttering forward and pulling on the handle.

The part of my mind that loves little details, hears the perfect tone of the car door opening. It's heavy but well-made and the noise it makes is one of quality. Like an airtight vault being opened. A slight suck as the seal gives.

I open the door wider, sliding into the leather seat, the smell of new car and expensive cologne hitting my nostrils.

Activating my other senses is helping calm my nerves, and with a steady hand, I close the door, the satisfying sound of it sealing shut makes my breath rush out from my lungs.

I'm not safe. I know that.

It only takes one look out the window, to see the two men who'd been chasing me down still standing just feet away. What happens when the driver lowers the gun?

"We're going to take this nice and slow," the driver calls. "I'm going to get in my car, you're going to go back to your boss."

"I don't think so," one of the killers calls back. "We need the girl." He's got an accent, but my brain is too frazzled to process which one I'm hearing.

"That's going to be a problem," the driver answers.

"For you." The other guy spits back. "Hand her over."

"Not going to happen." And then he levels the gun, I hear it rest it on top of the roof of his car to steady his shot. "New plan."

I've stopped looking at the men who were chasing me, my gaze now fixed on the driver. At least what I can see of him. He's familiar.

And his baritone voice has this rich, deep honey that reminds me of…

"You two are going to run. And I'm going to give you until the count of five before I start to fire. I suggest you begin. One."

Something on the gun clicks and it sends both of the other men into action. Reversing direction, they sprint down the street away from the car.

"Two."

"Three."

"Four." His voice raises with every number he ticks off, the two men moving further away until the first one turns down an alley, diving out of sight.

"Five," he bellows and then he swings into the car, weapon still in hand as he shuts the door.

In one motion, he tosses the gun in the back seat and then throws the car in gear, peeling out and gunning the vehicle down the next alley.

I gasp, grabbing the door handle as I realize I haven't even put on a seat belt.

"Duck," he grits out, taking a hard left as another gunshot rings out behind us. I hear the tink of metal as the bullet hits the car.

My head is between my knees in a second, my breath heaving in and out of my lungs as I try not to vomit.

Squeezing my eyes shut, the car picks up speed, turning right and then left, and then right again. "You can sit up now."

Slowly I raise my head, my breath anything but even.

I'm trembling all over as I swallow down a lump. "Are they following us?"

"No." he answers, racing down the street at what must be eighty miles an hour. I don't mind.

But the knowledge that what just happened is behind me, doesn't stop the trembling. If anything, I just shake harder. It's like some kind of delayed reaction that I can't control.

I have no idea how he manages it, but his jacket, still warm from his body lands across my lap. "Put it on."

I do as I'm told, automatically. I don't even think.

Pushing a few buttons on the console, the sound of a phone ringing echoes through the cabin of the car. I press my cheek to the cool glass. Maybe I should be worried about where we're going or what this man's intentions are. Instead, I close my eyes.

"Hello," another deep male voice answers.

The driver hits another button to transfer the call and then picks up his cell phone so I can't hear the other side of the conversation. "I need the boss now."

Boss? Who's boss? Boss of what?

I can hear the man on the end of the phone speak, but I don't catch the words.

"Pull him out."

More words that are too muted for me to make out. "Because. There's been an incident with Charlotte."

That has me sitting straight up. How does this guy know my name?

I look over, taking in the profile of the man I climbed into the car with, and my blood runs cold. It's Leo and Mason's youngest brother, Roman.

Older, harder than I remember, but the man next to me is definitely the youngest Kincaid.

I make some small noise in the back of my throat like trapped prey. Because I am. I've stepped out of the frying pan and fallen straight into the fire.

CHAPTER TWO

CHARLOTTE

THE CAR PULLS into an underground garage, the tires bumping smoothly over the speedbump meant to slow cars. We don't.

I'm gripping the handle again, my fingers clenched so tightly around the leather, my knuckles have turned white.

I haven't spoken since the call, and I'd hardly spoken before that. I'm not sure why, other than it doesn't matter. Nothing I might say is going to change anything that's about to happen to me.

Swallowing down my fear, I draw in a deep breath as the car glides smoothly into a parking spot right in front of an elevator.

Roman gets out, circling the car and opening my door. I could cry. Beg not to go inside. Mason warned me two years ago what would happen to me if I caused trouble. The limo ride after the incident in the club was the stuff of nightmares and they've filled mine often enough.

I know who Mason is. Yes, he's perfectly poised all the time because he's barely human. He's an animal, a predator. One I've been trying to escape.

And now I'm walking right into the lair of the beast.

Roman pushes the button on the elevator, the doors slide open. It's the first time, other than that very first moment, that I hesitate, but as his hand comes to my back to see me into the enclosed box meant to bring me straight to my death, I can't make my feet move forward.

"Please," the word comes out a soft plea. I know it's useless. The hesitation, the appeal for mercy, but I make it anyway. One feeble attempt at changing my fate.

"Princess," Roman slides his foot in front of the door to keep it from closing, the pressure of his hand at my back increasing. "While your please is very pretty, almost as lovely as your face, save them for Mason. Pretty pleases are your best chance for help."

I nod and step into the elevator, turning to watch the doors close and the parking garage disappear.

Roman hits the P at the very top of the rows of fifty buttons and I know we're heading for the penthouse. The elevator glides up the Vegas skyscraper. I should have noted which building we entered, where we are, but I'm not sure I care.

I'm bone-tired, but not just tonight. In general. Everything is a struggle and I'm not sure I want to fight so much.

The elevator slows and the doors slide open. I step into the large room, Roman's hand still at my back. The room boasts panoramic wraparound views of the Las Vegas skyline, the glittering lights set to a canvas of black filling the view of the floor-to-ceiling windows.

A configuration of tables is set up in the space in the shape of a U, thirty settings with half-eaten food and folders of paperwork littering the tables as though moments ago, this place was filled with people.

Now there is only one.

But he still fills the space.

Mason Kincaid stands in the center of the U like the king he is, fine suit accentuating the breadth of his shoulders. His arms are crossed, his height dwarfing me from fifteen feet away.

I stutter step in my sneakers, knowing that I was always building to this very moment. Why did I even bother to fight it?

I've got nothing left in my veins as Roman and I stop three feet from him.

I'm still in awe of this man. He's a bit older, a touch of grey sprinkling his temples. How does that make him look hotter?

His jaw is hard enough to cut glass, his brown eyes so dark they are almost black. The only soft thing about him is his mouth, full and sensuous, even set in a hard line, it's gorgeous and I find myself staring at this one feature. I'd like to trace its edges, know its shape.

"Charlotte."

My name on his lips does little to quell my fears. It's hard, rough, angry. Interestingly, it sparks a bit of life back into my limbs and I find myself standing straighter.

I must be a picture.

White sneakers, black mini skirt, Roman's leather jacket. No style points are going to save me. "Mason." His name isn't a challenge. It isn't a plea either. It might be a sigh. He's dominated the last two years of my life even though I haven't laid eyes on him.

And he still evokes this reaction no man has before.

"In the midst of trouble again."

I shake my head. "I didn't mean to be. Either time."

"That doesn't change anything." He bites back.

I know that. I know what he told me that night, too, when he'd slid into the limo, all muscle and sinew, blood staining his right cuff. The reason, the only reason, I was alive was because I hadn't actually seen anything. But if I caused any trouble, talked to anyone, they were the sort of men who eliminated trouble. Permanently.

And here I was in trouble again.

The one saving grace of that night was that Leo never called me again. I can only assume that he either lost interest or was told not to, but it had saved me from having to break it off with Mason's brother.

"I'm aware of that," I murmur back as I shrug off Roman's coat. It's a beautiful piece of clothing, the fine, buttery-soft leather sliding under my fingers as I swing the fabric around to my front. Carefully, I do up the zipper on the front and then fold the garment in half, laying the sleeves at a forty-five-degree angle. Draping the piece over my arm, I extend the piece to Roman. "Thank you for the jacket."

He looks down at it for a moment. "You don't have to return it."

But I hold it out further until he finally takes the jacket from my hand. It's then that I sink to my knees, closing my eyes. "And thank you for rescuing me from those men," I whisper. "I don't know what they would have done to me but I'm certain it's—"

"You don't talk to him. You talk to me," Mason grits out between clenched teeth.

I give a small nod. The carpet under my bare knees is plush and soft and I spread my hands into its deep fibers. "I just wanted him to know that no matter what happens tonight, I'm glad he stopped that..."

I'm not interested in upsetting Mason. Far from it. I force my eyes open, looking up at him. He always towers over me but down at this level...he's massive.

His gaze is hard and unreadable as his jaw works.

"And I remember what you said...that night..." I draw in a large gulp of air, making a silent plea for a bit of strength. "I just have one request."

"You don't get to request anything," he bites out rough and hard, his fists clenching at his sides.

I start, the volume of his voice making me shake again. I bite at my lip, forcing myself to hold his gaze. This is important.

He turns his back to me then, crossing to the table and picking up a crystal glass full of amber liquid. In one gulp, he swallows it down then lifts a decanter to refill the glass.

I can hear the pour, see the sparkle from the overhead lights as the liquor swirls about the snifter.

Full drink in hand, he comes back to me, where I've stayed on the floor. "You've made my life very difficult, Charlotte Fairfield. You know that, don't you?"

I nod, sure he's telling the truth. Some men can't be trusted to be honest. Mason isn't one of those men. He's too powerful to deceive. He doesn't need to cover the truth to bend people to his will.

A lion never lies to you. He just devours. "I know."

My shirt pulls across my back, cheap, ill-fitted cotton. It scratches at my skin and I barely keep from fidgeting. In this position, on my knees on the floor, the skirt has risen up so high, I can almost see my underwear.

Not that they're impressive. Nothing about me is impressive. Whatever swagger I had when I met Leo, it's gone. I just want to slink away and lead some quiet, simple life. But that isn't happening.

Which means I might as well go out with a bit of dignity.

"Mason," I whisper again. Our eyes meet and I force my back straight. "Please don't hand me over to those men."

His lip curls. "I don't have a lot of choices here, Charlotte."

Pulling one hand from the carpet, I reach toward him, as though touching him might make him more sympathetic. But I stop myself before I actually make contact. Other than when he held me that night at the club, we've never touched. I'm sure it wouldn't be welcome now. "I know. But…"

I notch my chin higher, forcing the words that had just died from my throat. "But if I'm going to die, I'd prefer you be the one who kills me."

Complete silence meets my request.

CHAPTER THREE

CHARLOTTE

"CHARLOTTE," Mason grits out again. But this one is different. Rougher. More emotional. His hands are under my armpits and he's dragging me to my feet.

He activates the fight that's pure instinct. Maybe the running had taken it out of me. I don't have much to begin with. It's why Gus can always get me to take the extra shifts.

Why I drank so much that night I wanted to end things with Leo.

But I've found it now, and as he pulls me up, I kick out, afraid of what he's going to do.

What he does, is pin me to his chest. Arms around me like a vise, one around the small of my back, one across my thighs, my boobs are pressing into his face. I could scratch at his eyes, but I've already realized the futility of fighting.

I'm never besting this man. He neutralized me in an instant. Not that he's hurting me. His arms are almost a comfort tonight.

My fight ends as quickly as it began and instead of raking fingernails down his face, I find myself holding his head in my hands, my fingers winding into the silky strands of his hair. I look down at him, tears filling my eyes for the first time tonight.

One slips out, balancing on my eyelashes before it tracks down my cheek.

"Fuck," he curses.

But I only dig my fingers deeper into his scalp. The strong hard planes of his body feel ridiculously good. Maybe I've gone mad, but I want to sink deeper into him. "Please," I beg. "Don't give me to them. At least if it's you I know—" My throat clogs and I can't get any more words out.

"Know what?" He sounds like the crunching of broken glass.

"It'll be quick and painless. You'd do that for me, wouldn't you, Mason?" I think I might be getting hysterical because my words come out between little puffs of air, my lungs struggling, and I'm holding him like a raft in a storm. "Please," I ask again. "Please don't give me to strangers."

His arms tighten about me, his hands spreading out on my back and bare thighs. "I'm going to put you down," he speaks slowly, like he might be talking to small child. "And you're going to stay right where I leave you."

I nod. I'm not running. There's no point. But I can't quite let go of him either, my hands still buried in his hair. There is a second thing about Mason that is soft. His silky mass of dark, wavy hair.

Without meaning to, I curl around him, my cheek resting on the top of his head. He holds still, allowing me this moment. I think I might be drawing from the well of his strength. I'm going to need it for whatever comes next.

Finally, he loosens his grip, lightly bending to set me on my feet. I try to relax my hands to let him go, but it takes me a second, two, to unclench my fingers enough to untangle them from his hair.

When I've finally untangled myself, he steps over to Roman, the two of them speaking so softly that I can't hear them. I only catch the low rumble of their voices, such a pleasant baritone that I close my eyes and just enjoy.

Men who are that devilish shouldn't be allowed to sound like that. Warm, rich, it's like the liquid in Mason's glass.

I open my eyes then. How did I not notice he'd set the crystal on the table two feet to my right?

Taking a step toward it, I pick up the glass and draw in the scent. Whisky. Really nice whisky.

Without asking, I take a sip, and then another. This isn't like me at all to just take something, but then again, today is not a normal day. It burns but in the smoothest way I've ever experienced, the liquid soothing my throat and spreading warmth through my body.

"Let's go."

I look up, Mason has joined me again, his body so close, I can feel his heat. Or maybe that's the whisky.

"All right." I start to set the glass down, but he reaches for my hand, wrapping his much larger fingers around mine. I wish I had my camera. The visual of his large hand engulfing my small one around the crystal snifter is stunning and I stare as he brings the glass to his lips, taking another drink.

Our hands still wrapped together, he brings the glass to my mouth. "Go ahead."

I take another drink, the liquid sliding over my tongue as my eyes flutter closed. I'm determined to enjoy every tiny, beautiful moment as I take one more sip.

He takes the glass from my hand and for a moment we just stand there, close but still.... I have no idea what he's thinking.

Finally, his hand comes to my back. "Let's go."

Do I even ask where? I don't. I just allow him to lead me back to the elevator and down to the parking garage.

When the doors open to the parking garage, I smile. "Hello, old friend," I whisper. He gives me a curious glare but I only shrug.

On the other side of Roman's car, the black sedan now sporting a nice new bullet hole, Mason opens the door to a limo.

He gestures for me to step in, and I do. I don't know where we're going...am I allowed to make requests? "I bet the desert is beautiful at night."

"Hmmm," he answers, not looking at me. He slides into his seat, his eyes fixed on his phone, darting over the screen before he begins to type on the screen.

I wrap my arms about myself, sliding deeper into the plush cushions of the seat. My eyes slide closed. It's comfortable enough that I could sleep right here. I think that whisky is taking effect, my body is so heavy.

But even at that, I'm still aware. It feels like we've hardly left the parking garage when we're pulling into another. I sit up, confusion making my brow crinkle.

Mason looks up at me. "I live close to work. Keeps commute times down."

My lips part as I stare. We're discussing commute times? But as soon as I have the thought, I realize its completely the wrong one. "Live? We're going to your home?"

He lets out a heavy sigh as he leans forward, his elbows coming to his knees. "You, beautiful little Charlotte, are a real pain in my ass, you know that?"

I blink, trying to decide what to say. Is there really a response for that? "Sorry?"

One side of his mouth quirks, making him look almost human. Still perfectly gorgeous but more human, as he sits back in his seat. "Until I've decided the best course of action, I'm tucking you in the safest place I know."

"And where is that?"

"My apartment."

I gasp, trying to understand that one. "I'm going to live with you?"

"Temporarily. It's probable that the goons doing the shooting have no idea who you are. It's less likely, but still possible, that they don't know who Roman is. If both of those are true…"

I stare at him. The last time I spoke to this man, he told me under no uncertain terms that if I breathed a word about who owned that club or my connections to the owners, I'd be face down in a gutter. Why was he not just killing me and calling it good? "So we're going to play house for a few days?"

His mouth hardens again. "No. We're not playing house. You are going to be a good little guest and give me a few days to make inquiries to all the necessary parties." He leans forward again. "And the better behaved you are, the more likely I am to forget this entire thing happened."

I can't control my shiver. Is it fear? Something else? I shake my head, my brown hair falling about my shoulders creating a curtain for my cheeks that are growing pink. What does he mean by those words...*a good little guest*? "It's not that I don't want to please you..."

His gaze is razor sharp. "But?"

I lick my lips, maybe I have this wrong. Maybe I don't. "It's just that I don't have much experience with men. Like at all..."

His gaze narrows. "Explain."

Didn't I just? "I don't really date."

"You dated Leo."

"Three dates."

His head cocks the side, as he assesses me. The limo has parked but we don't move. That's my cue to continue.

"One dinner out and then home early because I had an early-morning photography class. One family dinner which you attended. And one trip to the club."

"That's Leo, but there must be other men."

I shake my head. "A date here or there. But Leo..." I don't want to finish. Something in the way his muscles are tensing tells me I shouldn't. Is there tension between him and Leo? "Most men irritate me."

"How exactly?"

I'm not sure how much to say here. "I don't know." I do. "They are just often so..." Weak. Insecure. Obvious.

Mason's mouth twitches and he snaps open the door, stepping out before he reaches out his hand to help me out too.

It's another parking garage, another elevator. But behind me, I hear the clanking of metal gates as the entrance into the garage closes.

No one is getting in and that ought to be a comfort. But I seriously doubt I'm getting out either.

We make the trip up to yet another penthouse and the elevator opens directly into Mason's home.

I stop in the entrance of his apartment, awestruck once again.

If this is the place I'm dying in, call me happy.

It's everything I've ever wanted in a space. It's not the high-end finishes, or the amazing views, though both are out of this world. It's the energy that flows through the entire place. Quiet, positive, clean.

It's the way the kitchen moves seamlessly into the dining and then the living room. And the high ceilings. The absolute silence isn't bad either, something I almost never get in the city.

Walking by the massive island, I run my hand along the cool slab of granite, murmuring, "Quartz is far more popular these days."

"I like real stone," he answers, barely glancing at me.

I agree. Completely. I'd like to lay my cheek on the surface, feel its strength. Instead, I follow Mason down a small hall. There are two doors on the left and one on the right. He opens one on the left, walking inside.

I follow, but stop a few feet in. It's a bedroom. Decorated in muted creams, a large bed is in the center of the far wall, a vanity in the right corner.

"This is the closet," Mason opens one door.

I blink at him, looking down at my skirt. I have no clothes other than my awful uniform. The closet isn't seeing much use.

He moves to another door. "And the bathroom." I get a peek inside and nearly gasp at the large sink with miles of counter and a high-end tiled shower with two different shower heads that I can see.

As exhausted as I am, a shower to wash the sins of the evening away, sounds amazing. "Thank you."

He gives me a small jerk of his chin before he brushes past me, my body prickling at his proximity. Once he's gone, I step forward, touching the coverlet on the bed before kicking off my shoes and socks, letting the carpet scrunch under my feet as I pad to the bathroom.

"Charlotte."

I spin back around before I've reached the bathroom, my breath catching as Mason fills the doorway again before he pushes deeper into the room, tossing something white on the bed. "For you to sleep in."

And then he's gone. Leaving the bathroom, I walk back to the bed, finding a white T-shirt on the coverlet.

Lifting it, it unfurls in my hand. It's certainly long enough to be a nightgown. Without thinking, I draw it to my nose, inhaling the fresh, clean scent. It's a finely brushed cotton that slips through my fingers as I glide my hand over it.

I carry the shirt into the bathroom and start the shower.

Steam fills the room, the large space of the shower is only separated from the bathroom by a single piece of glass. I strip off my uniform, bringing my underwear into the shower with me. I have no idea how long until I'll have another set, and this is my nicest pair.

Washing them out in the hot water, I hang them up to dry and then I step in myself, the rain head pouring down on me somehow makes something unfurl inside me and my legs almost give. The water feels so good on a night that's been so terrible that I let it just wash over me as I sink to the floor, my hands spreading out on the warm tile.

Water rains down, plastering my hair to my face. I might be crying, who can tell with all the water, and I bow my head, letting it all mix together as rivulets cascade down my back and over my chest.

I don't know how long I'm there, but I finally get my legs under me and use enough soap to call myself clean. I get out and towel dry. Shrugging on Mason's shirt, I climb into the cool sheets of the bed.

Tomorrow, I'll decide how to navigate this new maze of predators I've found myself in. It must be five in the morning, but I close my eyes and give myself over to sleep.

Which is why I only dimly hear the clicking of the door.

CHAPTER FOUR

Mason

Part of me thinks I shouldn't be in Charlotte's room, but the much bigger part of me doesn't really give a fuck.

It's my house. And Charlotte is here by my grace. Her very life is mine to do with what I please.

And I've dreamed of this moment. A hundred times…maybe more.

I run a hand across the back of my bare neck and then down over my pecs. Charlotte had been pressed to this chest just an hour ago, her body fitting against mine so perfectly.

The very thought has my cock hardening. Then again, I've always had a hard on where Charlotte Fairfield is concerned.

The second I saw her all fresh and dewy on my brother's arm, I wanted her. It's the silky curtain of brown hair, big doe eyes that tilt seductively at the corners. Her pretty pink mouth is so full and fuckable and her tits could fill a man's hand, even hands as large as mine. And don't even get me started on her legs. Long and lean, they go on for days.

Her looks are what sparked the initial attraction. But I'd felt a pull like that before. Vegas is full of beautiful women. Granted, Charlotte is a natural beauty not the nipped and tucked variety, and I'm a man who likes true natural quality.

So yeah, Charlotte caught my interest from the first moment she walked into my father's house. We still meet there once a week as a reminder of what's important. Family. Staying together. What took that interest and made it knife sharp was the way she cast down her gaze every time I looked in her direction, the shyness of her smile.

I'd been a dick that night in the club two years ago and I knew why. Leo had been about to close the deal with Charlotte. Even that night in the club, I'd taken one look at her and I knew I couldn't stand to watch Leo date this woman.

Not that Leo and I needed more reasons to be at odds. My brother and I were natural enemies in some ways. Always vying to be the top dog.

So when one of the rival families, Italian mafia gangsters, had fired a shot in my club, I may have exaggerated the issue, used it to send Charlotte out of my life. And Leo's.

I didn't take her for myself, though.

For two reasons. One, no one should underestimate Leo. If I'm the brains of this operation, Leo is the muscle. And though his temper rivals my father's, he's got enough brains to be a real threat, when he isn't too deep in the bottle.

And two, everything I do is for the good of the family. Even sending Charlotte away. A woman like that could tear me and my brother apart permanently and then this whole house would crumble.

Unfortunately, ending Leo's relationship with her had not stopped my obsession. Nor had it curbed Leo's resentment toward me.

I'd had her followed to make sure Leo didn't keep seeing her on the side. But the reports I'd gotten from Jackson had been their own kind of drug.

Jackson was a man who'd been hired at the beginning, a leftover from my father's company, and he was ready to retire. Having him watch Charlotte was the perfect way to keep him on the payroll with an easy gig. It also allowed me to feed my obsession.

But apparently Roman had figured out what I had been doing. Why else would my youngest brother have been at the scene to rescue Charlotte? I wince.

That was going to be difficult to explain.

Walking silently across the thick carpet, I stop at the foot of the bed.

Charlotte hadn't even pulled the covers over herself.

I'd heard her in the shower as she'd cried and damn me all the hell if I hadn't nearly gone in. She needed comfort and nothing would make me happier than to hold a naked Charlotte. Touch her skin.

But my obsession didn't matter. My family did, and if keeping Charlotte alive was going to hurt them, I'd do what I had to do. Even now, I could see how Charlotte might be the perfect pawn to help me control Vegas.

My fist clenches around the handles of the bag I hold as my eyes scan down her body.

She is wearing my T-shirt and nothing fucking else. One of her arms is tossed over her head, pulling the hem up high enough that I can almost see...

Having her come here was so dangerous, so tempting. My eyes scan down the long length of her legs. I'd love to have those legs wrapped around my waist. I already know she'd feel so fucking good.

I force myself to stop, turning away and setting the bag on the vanity. I called one of my usual clothing boutiques and, despite the fact that it's the middle of the night, they'd delivered some necessities for Charlotte to use in the morning.

The perks of being one of their top customers.

Setting the bag down, I looked back at the bed, Charlotte stirs and curls onto her side.

The hem rides even higher and I can see the slightest bit of her ass. If I really looked, I could catch what's between her legs. But I don't, even though my cock is now as hard as the granite counters Charlotte had admired in my kitchen.

Instead, I walk back over, grab the covers, and pull them over her body.

Because Charlotte is more than an obsession. She's a temptation I can barely stand. I look at her face, so soft as she sleeps, and think of how she dropped to her knees in front of me tonight.

That alone might have done me in. Nothing had prepared me for how absolutely gorgeous she'd looked on her knees with those lips parted and those soft grey eyes staring up at me.

But then... She hadn't begged for her life, hadn't even cried. She'd just asked me to be the one to end hers...

My chest tightens at the idea of hurting her, every nerve reacting with a ferocity that surprises even me. She is mine to protect, not to hurt. The slightest snarl pulls at my lip. I could burn down the world to keep her safe.

I've got the money. The men. The power.

My business is legitimate. But my competition...not so much.

It requires me to skirt a fine line that involves using less-than-legal means when the Italian mafia and those Russian bratva assholes step their toes over my line. Occasionally, I have to use force to keep their feet on their fucking side.

And the Italians owe me a very old debt that will be paid in blood. Make no fucking mistake. They will pay.

I don't mind living in the grey.

But it makes me harder, stronger, and more cunning than all those fuckers, that I don't have to lie, cheat, and steal to get what I want. That's what I've always understood that they don't.

I turn away from the bed just as the phone in the pocket of my sweats chimes that the elevator to my apartment has been activated.

Only a handful of people can do so, which means one of my brothers, my uncle Jake, or my cousin Luke is on his way up.

If it's Leo, a shitstorm is about to hit my apartment. Which is why I close the door to Charlotte's room and come to stand in the middle of the living room, my arms crossing over my bare chest as I wait.

Ten seconds later, the doors slide open, Roman steps out of the elevator and into the hall that connects to the kitchen with Luke behind him. My shoulders relax slightly, not that this conversation is going to be pleasant.

The five Kincaids are the backbone of Kincaid Enterprises. We came together when my father died, and we are an impenetrable force that keeps the entire operation strong. If three of us are meeting, it means that there is a problem.

I'd like to say that Roman and Luke think Leo might be an issue, but honestly, the problem could be me.

Then again, what did Roman think I was going to do with Charlotte? Shoot her in the middle of the conference room?

Roman takes one look at me and grimaces. "Stand down, big brother. I'm not here to fight."

My shoulders relax a little at those words.

That is until I catch Luke's face. He looks pissed. "I might have," he confirms, tossing himself on one of my couches. "Do not tell me you're going to fuck over Leo for pussy."

But I don't even answer before Roman snarls, "That's not what I brought you here for."

Luke quirks a brow. "You got a thing for her too? How fucking crazy is that? All three of you fighting for the same woman?"

But Roman's eyes swing to me as he says to Luke. "She dropped to her knees, but she didn't beg for her life, Luke. You know what she asked for? She asked for Mason to kill her himself instead of turning her over to those thugs."

"Fuck," Luke spits. "She's got balls. I can respect that."

"Technically, that's not true." But I get his sentiment. And I agree. She's got more grit than most men I know. One more reason why Charlotte is special.

"If I'd been on the fence before," Roman shrugs, "I'm in the protect Charlotte camp." He's watching me, paying attention to my reactions. If Leo is the muscle, Roman is the reader. He never misses intentions behind actions and he's watching for mine now. And honestly, he's getting smarter by the day.

"I will say what I always say, and I'll say it to Leo too. I am in the *whatever is best for the family* camp. You all know what I've done in the name of family, and I'll do it again. And until I have more information, I have no idea what we're doing with Charlotte yet."

But that same feeling wells up inside me. That she is mine to protect.

I've been obsessed. Maybe I need to fuck her already and let it go.

Luke nods, rising from the couch. "This is good. This is all good."

"How's that?"

"You're still you, still our fearless family leader. Roman is the one advocating for Charlotte's life, which will make all of this easier for Leo. Because we all know how he can be when he's angry."

Truer words. "Do we know who was killing whom?" I ask Roman, not wanting to worry about controlling Leo's temper for the moment. I've got a war to win but first I need to know my opponent.

"Working on it," Roman answers. "They had an accent, but then again, they all have accents. They were in Italian territory, but it was a Luciano who was shot dead, so we might actually have an ally against the Italians."

That was interesting. "Good work." I scrub my hands down my face before I turn to Luke. "Send some men to Charlotte's apartment. Find out if anyone has been there and watch to see if anyone comes."

Luke gives me a quick acknowledgment by jerking his chin. "Will do."

I look back at my brother. "If they're new players, they might not know you, Roman, and they definitely don't know Charlotte." Which means the problem isn't a problem at all.

I can hope.

Both of them head for the elevator and I turn to my room. But before I enter, I pause, staring at the door across the hall. Because just beyond that slab of wood is the woman I've been wanting for actual years. The very thing I've been denying myself.

And I'm just not sure I want to deny myself any longer.

CHAPTER FIVE

CHARLOTTE

I WAKE to the smell of bacon. Padding into the bathroom I find a toothbrush…was that there last night? Brushing my teeth, I open a drawer and find a new hairbrush as well, that I quickly run through my hair before I splash some water on my face.

Checking my underwear, I find them dry and put them on under Mason's T-shirt. I don't have anything else to wear, and honestly, it covers more than my uniform.

Heading back out of the bathroom, that's when I notice the cloth bag on the vanity.

I pull it open, clothes and products fill the interior.

I'm debating a shower when my door opens. A shirtless Mason fills the door, instantly making my mouth dry. "Come eat."

My eyes lock with his as my eyes drift down the rippling muscles of his chest and abs. "You're brave."

"For what?"

"Cooking bacon shirtless," I answer, moving toward him and the smell of food. How long has it been since I ate? "Grease splatters."

He quirks a one-sided grin and then disappears from the door, leaving me to follow.

Stepping out into the living area, I can already see the table is set for two. A fresh bowl of cut fruit sits on the counter. Mason cracks eggs into a pan, the toaster pops, the smell of fresh toast competes with the bacon in the best way.

"Have a seat," he says, flipping the eggs out on to plates.

Last night I asked this man to shoot me. This morning he's serving me breakfast. Weird.

But I don't bother to share my personal feelings on the topic of Mason cooking for me as he sets a plate of food in front of me.

I dig in, the sleep and the food making me feel somewhat normal considering.

"Can you be ready in a half hour?" Mason asks, having just finished his plate.

I swallow down my bite. "Of course. But may I ask for what?"

He leans back in his chair. "We're stopping at your apartment to pick up necessities and then we've an appointment at a clothing store."

I shake my head, trying to wrap my head around all this. "Are we still worried about those men who I watched commit a murder?"

"Yes."

"So we're going out shopping?"

He doesn't look amused. And he's probably right. One of the major crime bosses of Las Vegas probably has a better handle than little old me on what's safe and not safe.

I'm sure very few women question him and it's not in my nature to do so but...I'd really like to live a little longer.

"First of all, we're going to the boutique when it's actually closed, so it's not really public. And second, if we're getting technical, you are staying here while I figure out if you are or are not in danger."

My eyes widen. There is a chance that I might get out of this? Memories from last night filter through my thoughts as I remember him telling me something similar. Somehow, that hadn't quite computed last night. Fear, exhaustion, and whisky had made my mind dull. "You told me two years ago, if there was any more trouble, that would be the end of me..."

Did Mason Kincaid just wince? "You've proven you can keep a secret," he finally answers. "And believe it or not, I'm not actually in the habit of going around killing innocent women."

I wilt into the chair. Mason Kincaid is going to protect me. Sort of. "And what happens if they do know who I am?"

"We'll worry about that only if necessary."

I look out the windows at the Vegas skyline. Nothing in this town is free. In fact, it probably costs more here than anywhere else. "And the price for this protection?"

He doesn't answer.

Slowly, I turn back to him, his eyes burning into me. Yeah. I know what he wants. And I'm pretty sure I'm game.

The thing is...I know the dangers. But I'm a twenty-two-year-old virgin because most men don't tempt me.

This one does. I blush, dropping my gaze.

"Half an hour. We'll talk in the car."

With a nod, I get up from the table, automatically picking up my plate, but Mason's hand reaches out to stop me, circling my wrist.

Electric shocks course down my arm at the touch as my chin snaps up, our gazes locking again. "I'll clean up," he murmurs, his gaze holding mine.

I give some sort of distracted nod as I finally tear my gaze away, my eyes dropping to where his large hand dwarfs my arm. I've always had tiny wrists and ankles, but he makes them look miniature as he flips my arm over, his thumb stroking over my fluttering pulse. Slowly, he raises my wrist to his mouth and then he lays the lightest kiss right on the vein.

Now it's my breath that's fluttering, my mouth dry as I lick at my lips.

That's his cue to pull me closer. "Charlotte."

"Yes?"

"I know we have history."

I shake my head. "Not really. Meeting twice two years ago..."

"I don't go around threatening many women either."

Mason wasn't a liar. He was too alpha to need to use tricks. But I was calling bullshit on that one. "Every part of you is threatening."

He smiles again but this grin isn't amused, it's wolfish. "Possibly."

He is slowly drawing me closer, enough that I have to take a step toward him. His hand slides to my waist as he leans down close to my ear. "For as long as you are under my protection, every need of yours will be met. Understood?"

A girl could get carried away with an offer like that. I nod as he closes the final distance between us, my belly settling against the hard press of his erection.

Yeah. I'm not imagining what conversation we're having. "All right," I whisper, my head turned to the side, my eyes closed.

"Look at me."

I do as he asks, opening my eyes and tilting my chin up. I can't control my breathing, my blood hammering through my veins. Looking at him like this is making my body hum with a need like I've never known. My hands come to his abs, my fingers pressing into the sharp ridges. "Mason?"

"Hmmm," he lowers his head, placing a light kiss on the corner of my mouth.

With the break in eye contact, my eyes flutter closed again. "I know I told you I haven't dated very much."

His mouth moves a little more to center but not all the way, kissing the right side of my lips.

"But I have to tell you that I've never..."

He stills, his mouth freezing against mine. "You've never had sex?" I feel his mouth moving against mine as he speaks.

I shake my head. "No. Never."

He's gone before I can even find my balance and I nearly fall with the loss of his support. I catch myself as I blink my eyes open to find him standing a few feet away looking pissed off.

I grimace as I cast my gaze down again. I should have known. Men like Mason want experience. But what does that mean for my protection? We were bargaining, weren't we? Had I misunderstood?

"Get ready," he says before he turns and heads for his bedroom, closing the door hard behind him.

I do as I'm told, going into my room and then straight to the bathroom to take a quick shower. Wrapped in a towel, I find the bag and begin pulling out the contents, carefully lining up the makeup on the vanity, the toiletries in the bathroom.

Picking out a cute skirt and simple top from the bag, I'm relieved to see an adorable pair of slides at the bottom of the bag. Heels are the last thing I want today, and my sneakers do not go with this skirt.

I don't have time to unpack the rest of the clothes, so I stash the bag on one of the shelves in the closet.

With five minutes to spare, I use a bit of the makeup, a little eyeliner to highlight the sexy tilt of my eyes and some lip gloss, which is the perfect shade of pale pink for my skin.

My door opens and Mason appears in an open button-down shirt and dress slacks.

"Ready?"

I swear his gaze takes in every detail. From the arrangement of the products on the vanity, to the amount of leg the skirt shows—pretty generous—but nothing like my uniform.

I stand from the vanity seat, taking one extra second to return the lip gloss and eye shadow to their proper spots. It just makes me feel better.

Walking toward Mason, he steps back to let me out of the room, but as I start down the hall, his hand comes to my waist, guiding me toward the elevator.

I can't even pretend his touch doesn't make me tense, full of a hectic energy that has no release. So I keep my chin up and stay silent.

He said we'd talk in the car. But that was before I mentioned I was a virgin. Should I have not told him? But Mason is not a man I want to keep secrets from, and I'm not interested in upsetting him. Still, in a game where my life hangs in the balance and there is a price to be paid, I feel like I just gave away a major bargaining chip.

I'm about to find out.

CHAPTER SIX

CHARLOTTE

I SNEAK another glance at Mason as the car we're riding in creeps down Interstate 15.

The silence is killing me.

Normally, I like silence. I don't need constant chatter to fill the void. But we've left so much unsaid.

We're not in a limo like last night. This is a sedan, also new, and also amazingly comfortable. Mason isn't driving, however, we're both in the backseat as the driver navigates the congested roads.

The older gentleman who is driving catches my eye in the rearview mirror and gives me a kind smile. That's a nice change.

It takes more than half an hour to make the five-mile trip to my apartment, Mason mostly texting on his phone. I'd hoped for clarity during this car ride...

I trust Mason to tell me the truth and I wouldn't lie to him either. When the elevator opened last night, I'd made my peace with death.

The longer this drags on, however...

Did I just forfeit my protection when I admitted I hadn't had sex?

But I know I have no leverage in this situation, so I keep quiet, clasping my hands in my lap.

It's not until we pull up to my run-down apartment that I realize Mason is going to see where I live. How I live. Does he know I've been totally on my own? When my dad died, that small bit of help I'd gotten died too.

I wince, looking down the street at the homeless camp that's cropped up along the chain-link fence that barricades an empty lot just down my street. A tent city of tarps, drugs, and crime, the smell of unwashed bodies wafts toward us from a quarter mile away.

My building is a stucco row of apartments, the stucco in major disrepair. Mine isn't even a full apartment. It's been split into upstairs and downstairs studios. Basically, it's the worst of the worst.

I took the downstairs one because it's cheaper, but it's had its drawbacks. The break-ins being the most obvious.

My cheeks color as I look at the place from his eyes.

I'm not ashamed. I'm graduating college—hopefully graduating college—with no debt. How many people can say that?

But still, I'm not exactly proud of my address.

He doesn't say a word as he slides out of his seat and comes around the car to open my door.

I smoothly exit the car, adjusting my skirt and then walk to the front door with my head high.

I don't lock it. It just makes people break the window to get in.

Instead, I created a hiding spot for anything valuable.

We step into the space that could almost fit into the bathroom I used this morning in Mason's apartment, but my shoulders still unwind as I step inside. Small as it is, this is still my place. And it feels like me.

There's a pale floral cover on the bed, and a small cream couch I picked up at a moving sale.

My counters are always neat, just a candle out, not a lot of clutter. Some of my photographs are on the wall, and I painted a mural on the bathroom door which was too awful to save without massive splashes of paint.

I look back at Mason and he's taking in every item, every choice. "Home sweet home," I say as I open my one tiny closet and pull out a duffel bag. It's the same one I left Nebraska with.

I open the drawers and pack in my neatly folded clothes.

He stands watching, not saying a word, as I cross to the bathroom, getting some of my favorite products from the shower and the counter. Most of what Mason bought me is better, but this stuff…it's mine.

Now for the reveal. Not that I'm worried Mason is going to steal from me when he knows my hiding spot. It's just that this is one of the few secrets I guard. Not even my friends know where I stash my money.

I come back out of the bathroom and set the bag on the floor. He's next to the bed, looking at a photograph on the wall. A profile of my friend Kim in the setting sun. The light glistens off her red hair, making the wild strands look like they're on fire.

"Very nice," he says, looking at me. It's the not the compliment but his eyes that have my cheeks heating. There is appreciation there. And considering we're standing in my tiny, run-down apartment, it makes me feel better.

"Thank you." I clear my throat. "Would you mind stepping a bit to the left."

"Why?"

"I need to move the bed."

One brow rises and then he turns around, pulling the bed back from the wall.

Brushing back the artsy curtain I'd used to create the illusion of a headboard, I reveal my hole in the drywall.

Reaching in, I pull out my camera first. I love this thing. Next comes some pictures of me and my mom when I was little. They're from right before she walked out on us.

Then, I pull out my old MacBook. I can't complete anything without it. Finally, I grab the roll of cash that's my ticket out of Nevada.

My bag is at my feet, and I stuff the roll in under the laptop, placing the camera around my neck. I let the curtain fall back into place and step back, nodding to Mason to put the bed back. He does, not even huffing like I would, and then I give the place one last look.

It's not much but I still feel a bit of longing as I look at it. If only I could rewind to yesterday, take the other path home, I would have woken in my bed.

What is all of this going to do with my plan to leave Vegas? I've been itching to get out and I'm so close…

Reaching for Kim's picture, I stuff that in the bag too.

She works at Rebel's too and I don't know how I would have made it through the last few years without her. I'm going to have to call her and tell her something. I've got today off but I'm supposed to be at work tomorrow.

And then there's my project. Mason and I are going to need to talk about that. I can't fail this class. Not now. Not after everything I've gone through to make it this far.

I remember the list I'd ticked off in my head when I thought Roman was going to shoot me. Graduating…it's one of the things I need to do before I die.

Mason carries my bag out into the hall as I follow.

We step back outside and I stop, looking down the street once again. This is the part of Vegas they never show. Lifting my camera, I take a picture of the entire camp and then zero in on a few homeless people I see regularly as they stand outside their tents.

Their faces are cracked and worn, their clothing filthy. They are still beautiful in their own way, and they deserve to be seen.

"What are you doing?" Mason asks. He hands the bag to the driver, who places it in the trunk, as he comes to stand next to me, his hand at my waist.

I let him guide me back to the car as he opens the car door and I take my spot in the backseat. He comes around and gets in too, the door closing with a satisfying thud.

Silently, I hold the camera out, the pictures I just took flashing over the screen. He didn't ask me to show him, I just do. And not because I'm proud of them. Taking those pics is my way of not completely letting go of my life. Of accomplishing one of the few goals I set for myself.

He grimaces as he nods. Does he understand?

The car starts rolling as the phone rings. He picks up, only saying the single word, "Yes?"

He doesn't speak for the rest of the call because he doesn't have to. He vibrates power. One of his hands is resting on his thigh, the grey of the trousers only accentuating the delicious roughness of his skin, the long taper of his masculine fingers.

I don't think. I just lift the lens to my eye and snap.

His eyes flick over to me, and I flash him the screen. One eyebrow rises but he says nothing as he keeps not talking on the phone.

Then he hangs up.

"We'll have to delay the shopping. Something's come up."

"I've don't need to shop at all. I've got plenty of clothes."

He grimaces but doesn't answer. "Jackson," he points to the driver, "will be at the bottom of the elevator all day should you need anything."

We pull back into the parking garage, both Mason and Jackson climbing out. Jackson gets my duffel while Mason opens my car door.

This time, when I step out, he doesn't back up and his body and mine are incredibly close as he rests a hand on my hip. "I won't be back until late."

I look away, giving a small jerk of my chin. There is little for me to do but wait. "Will we talk tonight?"

His fingers fan out on my hip. "Yes. We'll talk tonight."

I want to remind him that we were supposed to talk in the car. But I'm not sure what I'll gain from irritating him. "Should I make an agenda?"

He pulls my hips closer to his, the heat of his body seeping into mine. "What would be on this agenda?"

I lift my fingers between us and start ticking off a list.

"The likelihood of my death. The living arrangement until we know. My duties in your house."

"Duties," his voice takes on this dark, rich quality that actually makes me wet even though I hadn't actually meant that.

"I'm not very good at just sitting," I say, trying desperately not to blush.

"Anything else?"

"Yes. My visual arts course," I say on a rush of air. Can he smell that I'm aroused? I swear he can.

"Charlotte. That hardly seems important." And then our hips make contact, his erection pressing into the softness of my belly again. Is it supposed to feel this good?

"Now see, that's why it needs to be on the agenda. Because for me, it might be the most important one of all."

He shakes his head. "I'll see you tonight."

A limo materializes and then Mason is gone, sliding into the next sleek car that surely smells of new leather and feels like riding on clouds.

"This way," Jackson gives me a smile that crinkles his eyes in the nicest way. He hands me a phone. "My number is in here if you need anything."

"Thank you, Jackson."

And then, like magic, the elevator opens. I step inside, taking my bag from Jackson and pushing the only button available. P. I didn't even notice last night that this elevator is exclusive to Mason's apartment.

I try to calm my racing nerves. I've got a long day of waiting ahead of me. At least I'll have time to work on my project. That is if I can stop my swirling thoughts about Mason long enough to concentrate.

The man is an enigma that I desperately wish to learn. Not only does attraction sizzle between us but he holds my life in his large hands.

CHAPTER SEVEN

Mason

The short drive from my apartment to Kincaid Enterprises isn't nearly long enough.

The call I took in the car while Charlotte sat next to me…Roman.

It didn't take many inquiries to learn that Roman was recognized last night when he picked up Charlotte. The killers, who've been doing their homework on their Las Vegas competition, made contact this morning.

There's a new set of players in town who've been buying up real estate. Some fucking British upstarts who claim to be the direct relations of some titled wanker. They call themselves, the Dukes.

I don't give a shit what they call themselves. I'm the king and they will bow.

Distantly, I know what's got me in a twist. Fucking Charlotte. That skirt looked beyond gorgeous exposing the exact right amount of her lean legs, hugging the curve of her hips and ass. And her place…

We'd driven up and I'd wanted to hate it. It was a run-down shithole. I knew where she lived already, but I'd never been there. Then we'd stepped inside.

Every inch had been made beautiful from her touch. From the painted bathroom door to the pictures on the wall, to the exacting nature by which she kept the place clean and tidy.

I'd stood there and wondered what it might be like to be a different man. I never wondered that shit.

But what if…

What if my father hadn't collected up a mountain of debts and then gotten himself killed by the Italians? What if I hadn't had to bail out his debts to protect my brothers? What if I hadn't had to use my law degree to become the real estate tycoon of Las Vegas with shady crime ties?

I could have been a regular guy with a woman like Charlotte. We'd get some shitty apartment, nicer than that one because I'm a damned hard worker. But Charlotte would take any place and make it beautiful. Turn it into a home.

Because she loved me. Wanted to take care of me in the way a woman took care of man. That had never occurred to me before. That a woman could make your life…beautiful.

Instead, I'm the guy with an empire that is surrounded in darkness. I have all the money in the world to give a woman like Charlotte and no life with which to provide.

I shake my head as I step out of the limo.

This is a dangerous line of thinking and one I need to shut down. We've got a meeting to discuss the next steps and unlike this morning's little conversation with Roman and Luke, the entire family would be joining today, including Leo.

The Dukes making contact mean that decisions have to be made and Leo is part of that. Always.

And I can not afford to be soft in front of my brother, or anyone in the family for that matter. My strength and attention keeps us all together. Protects us. I can never forget what could happen if I allow myself to be distracted. That was how my father had ended up dead.

I'm their leader. The man who has taken them down this road. It is my job to see them safely to the other side no matter the consequences or my personal preferences. And that includes Charlotte.

I step into the elevator, shaking off the mood that pulled at me. I need my war face.

The doors slide open, my gaze sweeping over the room.

Everyone has assembled. My uncle Jake, who is only a few years older than me, lounges in a chair, his feet up on the table, forever the gangster. He was part of my dad's crew before he was in mine.

I focus on the legitimate end of the business. It keeps us on the right side of the law and it keeps us earning big money. My dad wasn't like that though, and Leo takes after him. Rough, ill-tempered.

Though Leo got way worse after my dad died. I sometimes wonder if he'll ever go back to old Leo. Leo that was happy. More balanced.

Leo, Roman, and Luke stand to one side, Leo's face near mutinous as his gaze slashes to mine.

I had assembled a team of five for a reason. Being an odd number meant no tie votes under any circumstances. We made decisions decisively and then put them into action.

Leo and I rarely voted on the same side of any vote, and it didn't take much to see that we wouldn't today.

I love my brother, but he is a loose cannon that I always have to keep from going off...

Which means I have to persuade the rest of my family today. Because I never override a vote. It would undermine the other men in a way that would only breed dissent. We were in this together.

But if I hoped to argue for Charlotte to receive our protection, I'd have to be pretty damn convincing.

Leo looked ready to take a machete to the room. And I seriously doubted I had Luke's vote.

Roman was on my side. That left Jake as the swing...

"Tell us what you know," I say to Roman, taking my seat in the center and leaning back in my chair. Like I'm not crawling out of my skin.

Roman and Luke do the same, coming around the table and taking their seats. But Leo doesn't sit.

We're the same height but Leo carries more bulk than me. He's flexing it now, his gaze slashing into mine. I look away, slowly, like I'm bored. He's my brother and I'd die for him. I respect him too, but he's not the king here. I am.

It pisses him off.

Roman leans his elbows on the table. "I got the call this morning from Ethan Cunningham. Lord Ethan Cunningham, to be precise. Slick fuck with his smooth accent and his posh manners. Said things like, *I'm sure we can come to some sort of agreement chap,* and *we respect* blah, blah, blah. Long and short, they don't know who Charlotte is, just that we have her. They want us to turn their witness over to them." He sits back in his chair, his face hard in a way I don't usually see. Roman is growing into a man. For the second time today, I wonder if all three Kincaid brothers have a hard-on for Charlotte.

I'm not asking.

"That it?"

"Nope. Said their beef was with the Italians and that they'd happily leave us out of everything."

"As long as we hand over Charlotte," Leo says, leaning against the table. "Sounds easy enough."

My gaze swings to him. "Sending a woman to her death sentence is easy?"

Leo's face hardens.

"And besides, since when do we make a practice of allowing upstarts to make the rules? We don't allow anyone to tell us what to do. Ever."

I see my words sway the other men. They know I'm right.

"If I say that I have their witness well in hand, then the Dukes, out of proper respect, ought to take me at my word and leave the issue be."

Jake scratches his chin, and I can see he agrees with my argument. It's old school in a way he likes…

Leo's lip curls. "Maybe we should vote on whether or not to turn—"

Roman stands too, his eyes sparking fire as he glares at Leo. "We're not voting on her life."

Every eye is on him now.

"I've got to meet this girl," Jake says, pulling a cigar out of his pocket and lighting it in the conference room. He sets the sprinklers off regularly, but the fucker lights up anyway.

Roman's hand slashes through the air. "It's not like that." His gaze goes back to Leo. "She begged Mason last night to take her life instead of handing her over. She's got a warrior's heart and that's not the kind of person you just toss away, Leo."

"You respect a woman? That is interesting…" Jake grins around his cigar. "More interesting than you wanting to fuck her, that's for sure."

Roman's lip curls. "We don't make decisions with our dicks. It's Leo who is forgetting that. Not me."

"We don't need to vote. Not yet." I pick up a pen standing it on the desk, sliding my fingers down its surface. When I reach the bottom, I flip the pen and start at the top. It's calming and distracting. "I've nearly got the permits for the tunnel that will cut the Italians out of the chain of casinos. If I get the job done, we'll make a different kind of deal with the Dukes. One where they forget Charlotte exists and we give them some part of the Italians' bones to pick. It will be a win-win."

The casinos are connected by above-ground walkways. But I'm about to get digging rights. And when I do, the Italians are going to take a real hit in earnings, their traffic being seriously diminished. That's when I'll call in my debts and buy them out.

"And Charlotte?" Leo asks, his teeth clenched and his jaw hard. "What are you going to do with her while you haggle digging rights?"

"She stays put for now. No one speaks a word about her."

Leo moves so fast, if I were a different man, I wouldn't be able to react. He vaults over the table landing next to my chair.

But I see it coming and push out of the seat, standing to face off with him on even ground. He leans forward, his face an inch from mine as he spits. "She should be staying with me."

Now we were at the heart of the problem.

Leo is still pissed I cock-blocked him two years ago. He knows how to hold a grudge, and in this one, I can't blame him.

I've never put my desires before my brothers and he knows I did this time. Knows there has been a shift. It's dangerous ground because I've never done it before. Those kind of moves were for my father. And how he'd ended up dead.

Which is why, I never let that shit happen. But Charlotte's the kind of beautiful that can make a man froth. Pit them against one another. Even brothers.

Maybe I should give her up to him. He was the one that asked her out and brought her around. "No." The word rips from my mouth before I can hold it back.

Roman is now standing next to us like a referee in a boxing match. "She's staying with Mason," Roman answers quietly backing me.

I'm not certain why Roman is on my side in all this, and it's not the time to ask.

Leo turns his head, his face now in Roman's, the veins of his neck popping out. "Who the fuck are you to decide anything?"

Roman's brows cock as he eases back. "The man who rescued her."

Silence falls as those words sink in. Roman chose to bring her to me because he agrees that's where she belongs.

She does. I can feel that now. But I can also feel some loyalty shifting with Leo in a way that is so dangerous.

"Don't worry," Luke calls from his seat at the table. "Mason will give her up if it's in the best interest of the family. We're all still clear on where our allegiances lie."

"That so," Leo answers, his voice smooth velvet. Which is much worse than when he's spitting and yelling. "I want to hear that from his lips. Mason?"

"I will do whatever is necessary to further this family's business. But like I said, I don't think looking weak and giving her to the Dukes is the right move."

"But you would? If you had to?"

I hate the word, but I know I need to say it. "Yes."

"Good to know." He smirks back at me.

"Don't do anything stupid, Leo." I'm not playing. Leo is a weapon and turned against us...

But he's pivoting away, striding for the elevator. "Keep working on your tunnel. Good plan *big* brother."

And then he pushes the button, the doors slide open. He steps inside, crossing his arms over his massive chest. He glares at each one of us before the doors close and he disappears.

"You boys pissed him right off," Jake says around his cigar.

Luke scowls. "This is a chick he dated two years ago, a couple times. What's the fuss?"

I know the answer. He's pissed because I got in his way. Because I'm not following the rules we established when we started this business. I'm not acting in the best interest in the family. I'm thinking with my dick.

But it's Roman who responds. "Charlotte came to family dinner, took one look at Mason, and lost all interest in Leo."

"Ah," Luke pushes up from his seat. "Leo does not take ego blows well."

But I turn to look at Roman. Because this is news to me. "She hardly looked at me at that dinner."

"That's right. She looked at everything but you while you stared at her like she was a wagyu steak you'd just imported."

"And you've stayed away for two years? Your self-control has always been astounding." Luke looks at the elevator. "Still. Leo is going to be tough to manage."

"Just claim her," Roman says to me quietly. "And then we'll deal with the fallout. In between might be worse."

Roman was getting smart as fuck. I clap him in on the shoulder. "You know I can't do that. It goes against everything we've promised."

"We never promised to stop fucking," Jake rumbles the words. "Might do you good to clear out some of the cum."

He's not wrong. "Luke, can you to talk to Leo? He's not going to speak to me now, and I'm afraid his temper will get the best of him."

"On it, though I don't know how I'm explaining that we've agreed you should fuck her brains out. But...I'll think of something."

I start for the elevator, glad this meeting wasn't worse. No one threw a punch and the other four of us are on the same page. But I can't linger. I've got a ridiculous amount of work to do and even less time to do it.

And the faster all of this gets done, the better.

I mull over Roman's words as I take the elevator one floor down to my office. Just claim her…

As usual, things with Charlotte are not that simple. Still, the idea has merit.

CHAPTER EIGHT

CHARLOTTE

I HIT SEND ON my email, my body wilting into the chair. I did it.

I didn't have as many pictures as I'd hoped but I'd created a visual arts campaign on the dark side of Vegas.

Sure, I was a marketing major, and these pictures would never be featured in any glossy advertisement for the city, but that wasn't the purpose of this class anyway.

We were supposed to tell a story with our pictures. I'd started with glossy shots of the strip and then I'd transitioned to grittier and more derelict images, ending with the homeless. I'd even taken one trip down into the tunnel to show the tunnel people. It was a true portrait of all walks of life in the City of Sin.

I know I've nailed the assignment and all I can hope is that Professor Burke passes me based on the merit of my work.

The disgusting pig had cornered me in his office and went so far as to tell me I didn't need to do the assignment at all if I did some other things instead.

When I said no, I went from getting A's in his class to F's, so it's not guaranteed that he'll do the right thing now.

But I did my part…

I look up, realizing the sun has set, the lights of the strip filling the view out the windows.

Stretching, I check the kitchen clock, amazed that it's nearly nine. My stomach gives a hungry growl even as the elevator lights up, alerting me someone is on their way to the penthouse.

Mason appears a moment later with a bag in hand. "Tacos?" he says lifting the bag.

"Yum," I answer closing my laptop and heading for my room to put the device away.

"What were you doing?" he asks. I can hear him pulling out plates, opening the bag. I still. Was he worried that I was sending messages to people I shouldn't?

I pick up the device again, returning to the kitchen where I open the computer. I fire up my presentation, putting it on slideshow. "The purpose of the assignment was to tell a story with only visuals," I say as he serves me a shrimp taco that looks absolutely delicious. Fresh avocado, bright red tomatoes, and crisp romaine decorate the large pink shrimp.

"We're back to the agenda?" he asks, grabbing the plates and bringing them to the table. Then he returns to the kitchen, pulling a bottle of white wine from the fridge and snags two glasses.

I sigh as I wait, knowing the wine will be as amazing as the food in front of me.

His eyes flash to the screen, watching several pictures slide by before he returns to the table. "Your eye is exceptional."

"Thank you," I blush as I look down, listening to the delicate splash of the wine into the glass.

If most of the world is an assault to my senses, Mason's home is a salve.

"But I wasn't showing you the slideshow to start on my agenda, I just wanted you to know what I was using the laptop for. I didn't message anyone other than an email to my professor to turn in my assignment."

He pauses before he sets the glass in front of me. "I appreciate the update, and though you have proven yourself trustworthy, certain developments do require us to be extra careful."

I tense at his words, fingering the stem of my glass. "Developments?"

Mason looks tired. "Let's eat first."

I pick up my taco then, taking a bite as flavor explodes in my mouth. But I don't enjoy it the way I would have a few minutes before. What's happened?

Mason eats slowly, carefully, taking several sips of his wine. When he's done, he gets up to get another taco. It can't be too bad, can it?

"Another?" he calls to me.

"No, thank you." I wouldn't eat a second either way. I don't have a big appetite. But now, I'm nervous.

He sits back down. "Does that project mark the end of your college career?"

"Yep. And provided I pass, I will be the first person in my family to graduate from college."

He looks up at me then. "There are a few bits to unpack there. Why wouldn't you pass?"

I grimace, not sure how much to tell him. He's already dealing with a really big problem of mine.

But I've done that thing where I've looked down at my plate and Mason knows that means something is wrong. A finger under my chin makes me look up, our eyes meeting. "Tell me, Charlotte."

"My professor doesn't like me." I start but it isn't true. "Actually, he liked me enough to suggest that I..."

I don't finish because Mason lets out a rumbling growl that hums through me. I'm not scared though. I called Mason a predator, and I meant it. But he's my animal in this moment, and I appreciate having a beast in my corner.

"And you said no."

"I did. And I've been getting F's ever since."

Mason stares at me, his gaze dark and unreadable. "Let him give you an F on that project. He'll answer to me."

A smile creeps onto my lips. I've been afraid of Mason for a long time. Attracted too…but still afraid.

I never considered what it might be like to have the predator work for me…

It was interesting.

"Agenda item one accomplished," he said, sounding far more like the CEO and less like a gangster who cleaned up bloody scenes at clubs.

I have no idea what happened that night, and I'm not asking. "The other item we said we'd discuss is the cost of protection…" My face heats at my words. Fear aside, I've got a few bucket list items. If my life is in danger, graduating was one big one. But having sex with a man like Mason…

It's a definite do-before-I-die kind of task. Who wants to die a virgin?

Mason sits back in his chair. "The men who committed the murder you witnessed recognized Roman."

My gasp fills the space between us. This is bad. Really bad. "Is he all right?"

Mason gives me a small smile. "Roman is more than all right. He's growing into a man fit for a kingdom."

My shoulders deflate, relief moving through me. While my feelings about Mason are somewhat gray, I'm well aware that Roman saved my life and has asked for nothing in return. "Thank goodness."

"The men who contacted him don't know who you are, but they want to find out."

"Oh," I whisper. I was right to be worried.

Mason reaches out then, taking a strand of my long brown hair between his fingers. "It's time for a makeover, I think."

"Makeover?" This completely confuses me.

"Mmm," he rubs the hair between his thumb and forefinger. "Revamping your image can confuse your enemies and disguise your intentions. And in this case…hide your very identity."

My eyes go wide as I hold my breath, waiting for his next words.

"No more Rebel's waitress, which is what those men saw. You are now the posh and sophisticated girlfriend of Mason Kincaid."

My brows rise. Instead of turning me over to them, he's going to give me a makeover? He's always been full of surprises, but this one shocks me still. "You can't mean to pass me off as your girlfriend?"

"You're right. Not enough..."

I just stare, my lips parting. That's not what I meant at all.

"I'll have a hairdresser and makeup artist here first thing tomorrow morning. And that shopping trip we had planned for today—"

I hadn't planned anything. "You don't need to buy me more clothes."

He raises up one hand. "We've been dating for six months. You've been living with me for two and things have gotten serious. Very serious."

I blink at him, attempting to keep up. We really are going to play house. But are we going to play it all the way? "Mason, thank you."

"Don't thank me yet," he leans forward then, his hand slipping down my shoulder, over my arm, to grasp my hand. "If we're going to do this, we need to appear like a very intimate couple."

My blood rushes in my ears as I wait.

He's touching me again, his fingertips skimming up the inside of my arm toward my elbow. "You were right. There is a price for my protection."

"What is it?" I ask, hardly able to breath.

"I want your virginity."

And I want to give it to him. But somehow, him speaking those words has me shifted in my seat.

It's so transactional. This whole thing makes me uncomfortable. "Mason."

He laces his fingers into mine, leaning even closer. He knows when to speak and when to be quiet. Mason is impeccably perfect with even the smallest choices, and I find myself gripping his hand tighter.

There isn't even really a choice. Have sex with the sexiest man alive or be thrown to a rival group of gangsters and certain death. *Hmmm. Let me think.*

I cast my doubts aside as I square my shoulders. By way of answer, I loosen my fingers from his and push back from the chair.

Standing in front of him, I pull my shirt over my head.

I'm wearing one of the bras he bought for me, black lace demi cup that shows the smallest peak of nipple and pushes my boobs up and together for all sorts of cleavage.

Mason stands too, stepping closer to me, his eyes sparking, the tension and power rolling off him as he hooks his hand around my waist and pulls our bodies tight together. "Is that a *yes*?"

Tentatively, I jerk my chin in confirmation. I know I want this. But I'm scared too. I just found out that those men are one step closer to knowing who I am, and let's be honest, I've just agreed to have sex with the man I've been trying to escape from for two years. That's been different for all of two days.

He swoops his head down, capturing my lips with his in a kiss that sends my head spinning. It commands, it claims, and my body melts into his, wanting to belong to him.

His other arm is around me, his hands spread out on the bare skin of my back. His strong touch helps me to forget my fear.

But before I know it, he pulls his mouth away again. I stare up at him confused as he leans down and places a feather light kiss on my collarbone.

Then he slowly lets me go, taking a step back. I stare at him in confusion, my arms dropping to my sides. "I don't understand."

"When I fuck you, sweetheart, you won't be afraid." His eyes are dark and possessive, his hands clenched into fists at his side. "When I fuck you, you will beg me to be inside you and then you'll beg me to make you cum."

And then he stalks off, stomping into his bedroom, leaving the food and the dishes out.

I stare at them, trying to process all that just happened. Why does he care about my pleasure if I'm just giving myself to him as payment?

Slowly, I pick up my T-shirt and put it back on. Then I carry the plates to the sink, rinsing them and loading them in the dishwasher. I take the leftover tacos and pack them in the refrigerator because I'm too poor to waste food.

When I'm done, I wipe the counter and straighten the kitchen before I pick up my laptop and head to my room.

I've stayed busy all this time because I can't even process his words. Mason is a contradiction that I can't puzzle out. Is he my greatest danger or my one salvation?

What was it about him walking away that makes me want him even more?

Would he take me if I begged right now? I think I might be ready.

CHAPTER NINE

CHARLOTTE

I WAKE up to knocking at my door. I open my eyes confused. It can't be Mason, he always just walks in.

"Charlotte?" He calls from the other side. Apparently, he's knocking now. Did agreeing to be his fuck buddy upgrade me to knocking status? I would have thought we'd actually have to do the deed for that kind of consideration.

"Yes?" I call back.

"The stylist will be here in an hour. Breakfast is nearly ready."

"Be right there." I push up out of bed and start toward the bathroom. I hear the door open to the bedroom and stop halfway there because I slept in his T-shirt again. I might be addicted.

It smells like him still or at least his laundry detergent, and the fabric is so soft. But more than either of those, I know it makes me feel closer to him. This shirt was on his body and now it's on mine.

He sees me and stops, his eyes running up my body. "I did buy you night clothes."

"I know. I unpacked them in the closet. Thank you."

"And yet you continue to wear my shirt."

I look down, my hands running over the fabric. "It's very comfortable."

"You cleaned up the kitchen. I have a woman who does that, you know."

Did he? She must be very discreet. "I don't like leaving messes."

"I know," he answers, moving closer. He's in nothing but sweatpants again that sit low on his hips revealing a wealth of rippling abs. The sway of his body is even more fluidly beautiful in that animalistic way than when he's wearing a suit. I lick my lips and then swallow down a lump.

He stops in front of me, close enough that I could run my hand over his rippling stomach. I have the same feeling that I might be willing to beg him if he'd just kiss me again like he did last night.

He collects up my hair in one hand, letting the strands slip though his fingers. "I hate the idea of changing the color, but we can go with a long bob and a sweep of side bangs to give you a different look."

"Did you just say sweep of side bangs?" Who was this man?

He smiles. "You've got a great deal of natural grace and the sort of looks that make you easy to transform."

I still can't believe he is going to pass me off as his live-in girlfriend. Make it look like I couldn't be that waitress in the alley because I've been here for some time, living with him. Sleeping with him... The very fiction of it has me heating in all the right places.

"Sounds good to me," I answer.

His brow cocks as he twists the strands around his hand. "No complaint? Most women don't like a man telling her what to do with her hair."

"I trust your judgment." I mean the words. More and more.

He pulls on my hair the slightest bit. More tension than anything else. It's not hard and since he's holding all the hair, it doesn't hurt. In fact, it feels a bit more like a massage. But my chin lifts as my head tips back at his silent command.

He's so close that I can feel his heat and I spread my hands out on his stomach, loving the brush of his skin under my fingers, the ridges of his body.

He pulls a little harder, leaning down into my ear. "If we're cutting most of this off, this is my only chance."

"You'd better do it right, then." I say, not afraid in the least. My whole life has been tinged with a lot of pain.

It would be nice to have that mixed with some pleasure. And having my hair pulled turns out to be one of those things that has a whole lot of good.

I know it's so dominant, but in this, I trust Mason. He'd never push me past where I want. Hell, even last night he wouldn't touch me because he could sense my fear. He's a man of impeccable control, which means I can be whomever I want with this man and know that I am safe.

That is intoxicating.

He's still pulling, my neck completely exposed, and his mouth finds that spot where my pulse thrums. I don't even hesitate, I tilt my head to the side, making the hair pull harder but also giving him more access.

He makes the most satisfied sound as he kisses my skin, his tongue darting out to taste me.

Now I'm the one making sounds. A breathy little moan escapes my lips as I throb with a desire I never even dreamed existed inside of me. And all from a bit of hair pulling.

His other hand slides down my back, over my ass, giving it a generous squeeze before he's reaching lower, his hand skimming down the back of my leg to hook behind my knee and place my leg around his waist.

When he does….

His hard-on presses right into my throbbing seam and I gasp at just how good it feels. His lips are climbing up my neck like he's devouring my skin and I want him to kiss me so bad but also…I haven't brushed my teeth.

He senses the moment I stiffen. It must have been near imperceptible but he's easing back.

I already regret the thought. I didn't want him to stop. But he's backing away, loosening his grip on my hair.

My shoulders wilt as I pivot toward the bathroom but then I stop, twisting to look over my shoulder. "We could leave my hair a bit longer. Just below the shoulders."

Mason stops too, straightening up to his full height as he looks down at me. "I didn't scare you?"

I shake my head. "No. It was..." How do I tell him that he makes me want to push past every limit and try all the things because I know he'll hold the line for me whenever I need to stop?

"So what changed? Why did you shrink away?"

My lips press together. "Morning breath," I whisper.

For a moment his eyes widen and then he lets out a burst of laughter. "Take your shower, Charlotte. Breakfast will be waiting when you're done."

I rush into the bathroom, heading for the sink. Teeth first, shower second. It's on the tip of my tongue to ask him to join me.

I've crossed some threshold and I'm tired of waiting. But the stylist is coming so I shower instead and put on a simple dress that was in the bag of clothes. It's got a bit of stretch so even though it's fitted, it's also exceptionally comfortable. It's a pale pink that compliments my skin and the square neck shows a bit of cleavage. Putting on a pair of strappy sandals, I make my way out for breakfast. I don't bother to style my hair into its normal loose waves that frame my face, since I'm about to have them cut off.

Mason is dressed too, a suit today and he looks like the Mason I first met and yet... I've seen behind that veneer.

He's still perfectly intimidating but it's the kind I can't get enough of.

Fruit and yogurt are set out along with granola and I have a small bowl as Mason's phone rings.

He pushes a few buttons on the keypad and the elevator light comes on.

"The stylist, Hanya, and her entourage is here," he says with a smile, helping himself to his own breakfast.

"Entourage?" I repeat, gulping down a bite.

"I'll work from the table for a bit and then I might leave you to it."

I nod. "All right." But I'm not super thrilled being left with a gaggle of women who know each other. I have a few friends here, mostly just Kim, because I've never meshed with the Vegas crowd.

"If she asks about us?"

"Like I said…we've been dating for six months, living together for two, and things are getting serious."

"We're really telling people that?"

He nods. "That's right. If people start making inquiries, they'll go to people like the stylist to collect information. We sell this today. You're graduating and I'm giving you a makeover for a gift that spares no expense."

Mentally, I trip on that last bit. I've been living on a very tight budget. Not that Mason can't afford a haircut for me but still. I'm going to have to think very differently if I'm going to sell myself as the woman who landed the billionaire boyfriend.

"In that case…" I lean forward, my voice dropping to a conspiratorial whisper as I try her on, this new woman I'm to pretend to be. "I'll tell her, he pulls my hair like no man I've ever met."

"Charlotte," he grits out through clenched teeth. "I'm a man of incredible patience."

"I know."

"But you are pushing me to the brink."

Was I? Good.

The elevator opens and Hanya walks in with an army of women behind her. She is the exact sort of woman I would have expected to see on Mason's arm. Statuesque, blonde, and classically beautiful, her slender body is perfectly draped in her couture dress.

She smiles at me, a cold assessment, as racks of clothes get wheeled into the kitchen behind her. She claps her hands, her lips pulling into the slightest sneer. "We are going to have so much fun," she declares in an accent I don't recognize. It sounds fake. "We start with her hair, no? What are we thinking?"

Mason tells her his plan, Hanya nodding along as I'm pulled into a chair in the kitchen. "You agree?" Hanya asks as she breaks out her scissors. She hasn't looked at me since that first false smile, but her gaze does keep sliding to Mason. I can actually see the hunger in her gaze.

I understand. He's the sort of man most women would twist themselves into pretzels to have.

But at least for now…he's mine.

"Not completely," I answer in an equally conspiratorial whisper. "Leave enough length," I lean in, "so that it can be pulled…" my gaze slides to Mason, my meaning absolutely clear, "back."

Hanya gives me an appraising stare as she sizes me up, a little more appreciation in her eyes. "Very good." She's all business as she sprays my hair down and gets to work.

Two hours later, careful highlights and lowlights have been added to my hair, which now sits just below my shoulders, the cut angled to be longer in the front. There is a side sweep of bangs that somehow highlights my natural cheekbones and makes my eyes look even bigger.

And then Hanya starts on the makeup.

Mason interrupts to give me a very long kiss goodbye. It's soft and tender and I sink into it, trying not to lose myself. I know he's selling our story, and I appreciate the protection. But in this moment, what I'm grateful for, besides the kiss itself, is the look on Hanya's face. She's green with envy. "Have fun, sweetheart," Mason says, stroking a thumb over my cheek. "Buy whatever you want for dresses but get a few for upcoming charity events. You know how those are."

"Will do," I toss back, wondering what he's thinking. Why didn't he prep me for needed formalwear? I'm way out of my depth with the request. I can't even afford to shop at Forever 21.

But Hanya has been tamed and she starts pulling dresses from the racks that she thinks will work for this event or that one…

The morning and early afternoon pass in a flurry of trying on clothes, and dressing for every occasion. Leisure wear, out-to-dinner dresses, formal wear. The closet is full by the time the ladies leave, all babbling how generous Mason is to his girlfriend.

"You must come show us the ring," Hanya says in her parting shot, looking me up and down. "I'm sure it's coming any day and that it will be stunning."

Did she mean it as an insult? The only emotion shining in her eyes is raw jealousy.

It's late afternoon by the time they leave, and I sigh with relief. Tomorrow I'll ask Mason about ordering in groceries so I can cook.

I love to be creative, and I also enjoy having something to do. With that in mind, I pick up my camera, sitting on the couch, careful not to wrinkle the buttery soft skirt I'm wearing, one of the many pieces I tried on from Hanya's collection, and start scrolling through the pictures.

The phone Mason gave me rings, Mason's name flashing on the screen. I pick it up. "Hello?"

"All done?"

"Yep. Hanya and her posse just left. They managed to fill that massive closet."

He chuckles. "Not completely, I hope. We have another stop to make."

"Where?" I breathe, trying to imagine what else I might need.

"The jewelry store," he answers.

I stare at the screen, not answering. How did Hanya know? The light for the elevator comes on and my eyes dart to the doors. "Is that you?"

"It's me. I'll be right up."

CHAPTER TEN

CHARLOTTE

I STAND, my camera still in my hand, but other than that, I'm a completely new Charlotte. At least on the outside.

The makeup I'm wearing highlights every attribute while looking effortless, the clothes compliment my figure without being too tight or too obvious. And the way they feel…

Mason must know I have sensory sensitivities because every piece I tried on glided over my skin.

Or maybe all expensive clothing feels like that. My free hand slides from my waist down my hip just as the door opens. Mason steps into the kitchen but stops when his gaze catches mine.

"Charlotte."

My eyes slide to the floor. "Mason," I start, now completely overwhelmed. I'm literally covered from head to toe in gifts from him and this is an all-new feeling for me. "I don't…"

He's striding across the apartment and stands in front of me. Brushing his fingers through my hair, he leans in close. "You always look beautiful, but today…"

I feel my cheeks heating. "Thank you. For everything." I don't just mean the hair and the clothes. He spent that money to wrap me in a veil of protection.

He closes the distance between us, but this kiss doesn't devour. It's not full of animal passion. This one is light and gentle the way you kiss something you find precious.

My heart turns over in the strangest way to think of Mason Kincaid finding me precious.

I should not follow this feeling, it's going to get me in trouble. Other than wanting to take my virginity, the why of why Mason is doing any of this is a mystery to me. If I were a different woman, I'd ask.

Would it be better if I were more assertive? I've never been very good at that sort of thing.

I'd texted Gus to tell him that I wasn't coming in and when he'd responded that he couldn't cover the evening without me, I'd nearly caved. Only the idea of what Mason would do if I put on that uniform after he'd gone through a great expense to transform me, had me holding the line and telling Gus I wasn't sure when I'd be back.

Mason kisses me again, quieting my thoughts with the gentle touch and my eyes flutter closed as I sigh into his mouth.

If most women would twist themselves into pretzels, what would I do to really belong to this man? I'm not sure I want to answer that question either. Because I might do a whole lot more than twist, I might be willing to break.

His hand is on my back, sliding over my ass, pulling my hips into the cradle of his. My body thrums with need. He's right. If he keeps kissing me like this, very soon I'm going to beg.

He pulls back his face, the rest of his body still pressed to mine. "Ready?"

I shake my head. "You don't need to buy me anything else today, Mason. It's already too much."

He gives me that one-sided grin that melts my insides. "First, I've hardly spent anything. But second, if we're really going to sell you as the woman of my life, then you should be dripping in clothes and jewels."

I shake my head. So much trouble and expense.

But I let him lead me to the elevator, our hands entwined as we step in. There is something so personal about holding hands like this, I lift my camera, still in my other hand, and snap a haphazard picture. It's at an angle, our arms exiting the frame in the corners of the shot.

He looks over at me, his gaze holding a warning. I wince. "Should I not have done that?"

I flash the screen at him so that he can see what I've snapped.

"That's the second picture you've taken of my hand."

"You've got great hands," I murmur. He does. Strong, lean, masculine. I can't wait to see them sliding over my skin.

He's quiet for a moment, but I feel the energy. Nipping at my lip, I glance down. "I would never share anything that I thought compromised you or hurt you."

"It has never occurred to me that you might be a threat to my security."

My eyes go wide. Mason is a powerful man and likely a criminal. Of course, pictures might be a problem.

"You don't have social media," he says, "You've never spoken to anyone, not even your friends, about that night at the club."

How does he know that? It's a reminder that Mason Kincaid is a man to be feared as well as respected and desired.

"But I'm not sure I can allow you to snap pictures of me, Charlotte."

I nip at my lip. I'm not sure I can *not* snap pictures of him. He's magnificent. "What if I show you each picture when I take it? It doesn't even have to be your face. I just..." *I want to know you.*

He considers as the elevator doors open, and we climb into the car. Sliding into the limo, he sits next to me, his hand resting on my bare thigh.

Once again, I'm struck by the beauty. His skin is so much darker and rougher than mine. We're a study in contrast.

His phone chimes and he flicks down his gaze to read the text. I point at his hand and then wiggle my camera.

He looks back at me long enough to give a quick jerk of his chin in assent before he continues reading.

I snap his hand from a few angles, finally taking a picture that I think is just right.

It's a short trip to the jewelry store, the traffic less thick this time of evening. In another hour, the strip will be packed.

We pull into the back of the store through an alley and enter a door I'm certain most customers don't use. It leads into a private room that doesn't have cases of jewels.

Instead, pieces have been set out on a long counter.

I gasp, despite myself as a large sapphire cocktail ring winks back at me.

Mason chuckles, flicking a hand in the direction of the ring. "We'll take that one."

I hadn't even noticed the salesperson until the man steps forward with a nod.

"Might I suggest, this as well," he points to an aquamarine set of earrings and necklace.

"Not my preferred stone," Mason murmurs.

"But it suits the lady's eyes," the salesperson says with a flash of a grin meant to charm.

Mason nods as we move down the table. I mostly allow him to pick out the pieces. I know they'll be perfect.

The cocktail ring is slipped onto my right finger and the way it flashes and winks under the jewelry store lights is magical. It keeps drawing my eye.

"Any diamonds, sir?" The clerk asks.

Mason nods in the affirmative and my chin snaps up. I've already gotten a ring, two necklaces and two pair of earrings.

Diamond studs are brought out, "For everyday wear," the man says with a smile. They must be a carat and a half each. I don't know a ton about jewelry, but I know fat diamonds are expensive. "These fulfil all four C's where diamonds are concerned?"

I look at Mason, having no idea what the man means by four C's.

"Cut, Carat, Color, and Clarity," he answers my question that I didn't even ask. Mason is clearly very comfortable in this world.

We keep moving down the display, Mason's hand at my waist as he dismisses various items, chooses others.

At the end of the line is another ring.

I stop when I see it because I've never even imagined something so beautiful. It's a pink diamond in a platinum setting that must be over three carats in size.

"Try it on," the clerk has noted my reaction, and his eyes are sparkling nearly as much as the ring. Which tells me this piece is beyond expensive.

I shake my head. "No, that's all right. I…"

Mason's hand, which has been at my back slides to my hip, his fingers splaying out in a move so possessive, it has my nipples tightening. Does he have any idea how much his touch affects me? "I want to see it on your finger."

That starts my heart hammering in my chest, with something that isn't lust, it's so much deeper. Why this ring is different, I don't know. It's just so…me. Simple in design, perfect in its proportions, set in cool tones that compliment my skin, I just know I'm going to love it.

The clerk lifts my hand and slides the piece on my finger. The ring is already made to size.

I stare down at my hand, my fingers splaying out as a gasp falls from my lips.

Mason pulls me against his side, my hip pressing into his erection. I had no idea trying on engagement rings might turn a man on, but he is.

I look at him, my eyes surely swimming with questions, but his gaze doesn't answer them. If anything, his eyes are darker and more dangerous than I've ever seen.

I look away, slipping the ring back off my finger and then I reach out to hand it back to the clerk. I'm allowing myself to get caught up in the moment. This is not real. None of this is real.

But Mason's hand covers mine, stopping me from returning the ring.

My eyes go to his again. He still has a glint to his I don't understand, the predator I've always known lives in Mason right at the surface.

He takes the ring from my fingers and reaches for my hand, slipping the stone back on.

Only then does he look at the clerk. "We'll take it."

I look back down at my hand, the pink diamond sparkling back up at me. Is this part of how a predator protects or is he just garnishing his meal before he devours it?

Either way, there is no going back.

Somehow, this ring is the last step in allowing Mason to completely claim me and I am now his to do with as he wishes.

Maybe I have been for a long time. I've lived by Mason's grace for the last two years. But I'm less certain than ever how this will end.

CHAPTER ELEVEN

CHARLOTTE

I SLIDE into the limo expecting the rings to look duller in this light. They don't.

The diamonds are now nestled on each lobe and the aquamarine solitaire necklace is on my neck. No numbers were discussed, and I have no idea how much money Mason just spent.

When he mentioned me pretending to be his live-in girlfriend to create an alibi, I had no idea I'd be racking up this much debt.

The two thousand dollars I have stuffed in my closet at his apartment seems rather paltry for repayment.

Then again, Mason has already named a price...

"I want a picture of your hand," Mason sits next to me, his arm going around the back of the seat, his other hand wrapping about mine as he holds up our joined hands, the pink diamond catching fire in the sunlight.

We're palm to palm, but the back of my hand is facing us. I'm nestled into his front as I pick up the camera from where I left it on the bench. Then I snap a photo of his hand holding mine, the ring on full display.

I take the shot, showing him the digital screen.

"Where do you print these?" he asks.

My brows lift as I look back over my shoulder at him. "I don't think we're going to CVS."

"No."

"I have access to a high-quality printer at school."

"That won't be necessary." He picks up his phone, his arm still around me, my body still resting against his. I lean back, used to him spending his car time conducting business on his phone so I use my time to study the ring. The one I shouldn't love…

I snap another picture as the car leaves the alley and the light changes. Mason's eyes flash to the screen. "Better."

I nod, noticing the way the light is now slashing across his hand holding his phone. It's an everyday occurrence made beautiful by light, and I take the picture without thinking, and then another of his leather shoes, which somehow embody this rich, successful, dominant man.

He says nothing, surely noting the pictures as they flash on my screen. It's not lost on me that I seem to only take pictures of Mason these days. Perhaps he's the only subject to which I have access.

Or maybe, I'm obsessed.

He's still working on his phone, so I switch the camera to my other hand, and place my right on his dark trousers, my skin looking even paler against the dark fabric, the sapphire ring winking up at me as I snap another.

"Let me see," he rumbles and I show him, my fingers flexing against the muscles of his thigh.

He feels so good. Our eyes meet, my lips parting. I can't hide that I want more of him, that I want to feel that power he so effortlessly displays.

But the limo stops.

I look up, no idea where we are.

"Hungry?" he asks as the door opens.

We are once again entering through a back door into a private room where food has already been laid out for us.

It's American cuisine but it's ridiculously nice cuts of beef and fish in delicate sauces. We sit, a server presenting Mason with a bottle of champagne.

He nods and the bottle is opened, two glasses of sparkling pale gold liquid fills our glasses.

My brows lift but I say nothing until we are alone. "Mason..." I start my tone clearly letting him know that I'm looking for answers.

He takes a sip of champagne. "Not here."

"All right." I take a sip too and then help myself to a piece of fish. I trust him enough to know that if he says private affairs shouldn't be discussed, they shouldn't.

His hand slides across the table, taking mine. He turns it to study the pink diamond again. If I'm not mistaken, he's attached to the ring too.

But we don't say much as we quietly eat, our hands joined the entire meal. Is it for the staff? Do we appear the picture of a newly engaged couple? Should I discuss wedding plans? That's just too much for me...

It's the best meal I've had in years. Maybe ever. I like comfortable silences and this feels like one.

When the meal is done, Mason helps me from my chair, his arm around me as we make our way back out to the waiting limo.

When we climb in, he's right next to me again. "You didn't question me when I asked you not to speak."

I twist to face him. "In that situation, I'm well aware you know best."

He looks at me for a moment before he captures my mouth with his own. For a second, the kiss is tender, but in a blink, it's hungry, our tongues tangling together as I land in Mason's lap. I hadn't even noticed his hands had come to my hips until I'm settled in the cradle of his.

I press to his front, my breasts crush against his chest, my arms tangle about his neck.

He runs his hands from my hips, up my back and then down again, my body hums at all the contact.

The kiss is so intense, when he nips at my tongue with his teeth, it only makes me hotter.

His hand slides up my leg, under my skirt and over my thigh, my sex throbbing with the need for him to touch me. I'm ready to beg.

I don't even notice the limo has stopped until Mason pulls away and sets me to the side. Then, he opens the door. Usually, it's the driver. My head pops up as I look around in question. "Where'd we lose Jackson?"

But Mason only chuckles. "He knows when to be discreet."

That's a detail that bothers me. I'm not the first woman to arrive at this penthouse in the back of Mason's limo.

And surely, I won't be the last.

Have other girls tried to give every part of themselves to this man?

Likely yes.

I try not to think about it as he pulls me into the elevator, but I clearly stiffen and he feels that.

"Nervous, sweetheart?" He pulls me against him, his hand cradling the back of my head. It's romantic the way he's comforting me, and I relax, closing my eyes remembering that I want whatever Mason gives for as long as he is willing to give it.

This was never going to be permanent, and I should know better than to even wish.

"No," I answer, shaking my head. "I'm not. Today has just been…" A revelation? Of what it might feel like if this man loved me?

It's a fantasy but one I just want to sink into and pretend without interruption.

I know he wants me. He wouldn't have asked if he didn't, and clearly he's committed to holding up his end of the bargain. Of keeping me safe.

But where that ends and any sort of real affection begins, I have no idea.

I turn my brain off, or I try. His fingers are skimming down my spine. This is not teeth and tongues, this touch is silk and lace and I close my eyes and wrap myself in the wish of his gentle fingers.

If I concentrate, I can believe.

My forehead drops to his shoulder, my hands resting on his biceps as I draw in a deep cleansing breath of air.

One of his hands splays out on the small of my back, spanning from one side to the other as the other slides to my hip. But he's not pulling me tight against him. Instead, he's cradling me.

Like he knows I need some comfort. He probably does know. Mason's always been hyperaware of small changes in me, probably in others too. It must make him a lethal negotiator.

The elevator stops and the doors swish open but I'm not sure I want to move. I'd like to freeze this moment.

He brushes a kiss on the side of my head, murmuring some small word of comfort. But a second later, he freezes, going granite hard under my hands.

"Well, isn't this just fucking cozy."

Leo. It's been two years, but I recognize the deep tenor of his voice, so much like Mason's. Unlike Mason, there is no filter on his anger. I can feel the simmer of his temper boiling just under the surface.

It's Mason's control that makes me feel safe and I press deeper into him now. He gives me a quick squeeze.

The gesture is so fast, I might have missed it, before he's tucking me behind him, walking into his apartment. "I don't let myself into your place without permission."

Leo's lip curls. "This is what you might call a special circumstance."

"Why?"

"Because. My brother has decided to fuck me over."

I gasp, shrinking further behind Mason. He gives me a quick look over his shoulder and then reaches back for me, pulling me forward to his side. "Charlotte, go to your room."

"Is she a naughty teenager?" Leo asks but his eyes are all over me and I know he's taking in every detail. The hair, the skirt, the jewelry. "I take it back. Not a teen at all. You've turned her into a socialite."

Then his lip curls into a sneer. "Is she wearing a fucking engagement ring?"

"My plan," Mason starts, his voice barely containing his fury. "Is to play her off as a long-term part of my life, which would obviously mean she was not the cocktail waitress who witnessed a murder."

I'm looking between them, trying to decide what to do. I trust Mason and usually I follow his directives without question but to get to my room, I have to pass Leo.

Leo snorts. "That's a stupid fucking plan."

Mason looks at me. "Go."

I start to edge around Leo but I'm just passing him when he lunges out and grabs my wrist, pulling me toward him. "You chose the wrong brother," he snarls in my face. "I wouldn't pussy foot around with tunnels and haircuts. I would create a bloodbath to keep you safe."

Mason is next to us in a second, his fingers wrapping around Leo's wrist the three of us locked in an odd triangle. "Let. Her. Go."

"When did you become her keeper?" Leo barks back. "Come to think of it, how did Roman just happen to come to her rescue?"

I blink, how did that question not occur to me?

Mason bares his teeth. "I'm not going to say it again."

Leo squeezes my wrist and I cry out. Mason's face is in his face, his teeth bared, before Leo finally lets me go. I stumble back and then spin, dashing into my room. I don't stop until I reach the bathroom and then I slam the door shut, locking it behind me.

CHAPTER TWELVE

MASON

"WHAT THE ACTUAL FUCK!" I don't yell very often, preferring a quiet, lethal sort of rage, but I'm yelling now. An inch from Leo's face. It's been coming for a while. There's a part of me that likes to believe that I started it with what I did that night at the club, but I actually know the truth.

As a man who pays attention to the details, I can't ignore this one. Leo has been unhappy for a long time. He wants to be an alpha and he's been chafing under my leadership.

And if it had been Roman, I'd have given him more power. But Leo is too volatile, and I don't trust him.

He knows it too, which is why this fight has been brewing for a long time. I've been avoiding it, not because I'm scared of Leo, but because I know, once it's done, we might never come back from it. We might be done forever.

"You've got a ring on her finger?" Leo spits back, just as loudly. "You're really going there?"

"I've got two, actually," I respond because I've got nothing to hide and I'm not ashamed either, and now that we're here, there is no holding back. There was a part of me that kept away from Charlotte because of the way I'd gotten between her and Leo.

But I see it clearly now. Charlotte was never going to be his. And my brother and I…it's time to let all the shit out and see where we land. Roman was right about that.

And what I know for a fact is that Leo wasn't right for her. Never had been. And there can only be one boss in the Kincaid family and that is me. He can fall in line or he can leave.

"This is the same girl that yesterday, you said you'd sacrifice—" I punch him in the nuts before he can finish. Hard. He goes down like a sack. Pun fucking intended.

It's not something I've done to either of my brothers or anyone else for that matter, since I was twelve, maybe thirteen, but I can't have Charlotte hearing him. What would she think if she heard I told them she was a just a pawn to get what I wanted.

"What the fuck?" he groans from the floor, his voice high pitched like he's the one who is thirteen again.

"If she hears you and she bolts, what are we going to do then? Use your head, Leo." I love my brother, but his temper gets in his way. Often. One of the many reasons he's not fit to run this operation. He should know that.

He starts to get up, pressing one hand on the floor as he lifts his torso. "So what if she bolts? She was never our problem. Your priorities are so out of whack."

He needs to think in this moment, strategize more, not just react. I may have ulterior motives where Charlotte is concerned but that doesn't mean my plan isn't solid. "There is clearly a war going on between the Dukes and our largest competitors. The men we want to make pay for what they did to our father." I stare at him like this should all be obvious.

Not that'd I'd give Charlotte over to anyone. I said I'd do anything for my family, and I will, but I can accomplish this without one pretty little brown hair ever falling out of place. That is becoming clear to me now. Charlotte is not a pawn to be sacrificed.

But for right now, I need to manage Leo. He's got it in his head that I took his favorite toy, and it's time we settled things brother to brother.

An angry Leo is a problem far more dangerous than either pissed-off, murdering Italians or upstart, thumb-up-their-ass Brits.

I'm not going to tell him that I'm using Charlotte in this war, because I'm not. But if he takes that as an implied part of the plan then so be it.

Leo has got to stand down and today is the day.

Because Leo, he won't ever be king, but he could be the man who tears the castle down.

Leo slowly gets up, I don't help him. "I know Roman is siding with you, but that doesn't make you right. And if you don't make this right—"

I straighten up, glaring at my brother. "And you think I'm wrong?"

Leo's teeth clench. "I know you are. You can paint it however you want, but it should be me between her legs. That was my ass to hit. Not yours."

It takes everything in me not to punch him again. I know it's a problem that his words make me want to hit things. Charlotte should be worshipped, not used and thrown away. And any man talking about her ass fills me with rage. "Get the fuck out, Leo."

Leo steps closer instead. "I'm not leaving."

"Why not?"

"Fine. I'll go. But I'm taking her with me."

I stare at him. Leo is losing his shit. "Let me ask you a question first."

"What?"

"Did you think about her once in the last two years?"

Leo blinked at me, like he can't believe I even asked the question. "And how you screwed me over? Every day."

I grit my teeth together. "Now, see, that's thinking about me. Not her. Did you miss anything about her?"

Leo's brows scrunch in confusion. "What does that have to do with it?"

"You want to take her now, not because you want to protect her, but because you want to beat me. Which is neither in her best interest or the best interest of the family, is it?"

If Leo ever wants a larger role in this world, he's got to learn this lesson. Then again, the way I'm playing my brother right now, maybe I need to learn it too.

But at the end of this, I will make our business stronger.

Leo hisses through his teeth, "Fuck you."

"No. Fuck you. And fuck your ego too. And fuck your temper and you, you selfish prick."

He spins. "You think you're so much better than me, but you're exactly like him."

I go still. I know he means our father. "How's that?" I shouldn't have asked. I don't want to know.

"Letting pussy get in the way of your good sense."

The hit hurts. We never compare each other to him. It's a wound too gaping and the fact that Leo has done it… "And you? How are you *not* like him? Blowing hard without a single thought to the consequences? You're going to ruin us just like he almost did."

Leo is in my face in a second, a sucker punch to the gut that had me doubling over. But I take advantage of the position to wrap my arms around his waist, sending us crashing to the ground. He twists, getting in another good rib shot before he finally rolls away.

But when he stands, his face is blacker than I've ever seen it. "I'm done with you, Mason. Done being your lackey. Roman can do your bidding because I am out."

And then he stomps to the elevator. I watch him go, watch the doors close. It was bad, but honestly, it could have been way worse. Leo will calm down and then he'll be back.

Pulling out my phone, I see the video feed of him leaving the elevator. That's when I change the code. No one is getting in here again without my express permission, Leo least of all.

Firing off a text message, I set a family meeting for first thing in the morning, knowing that I'd better have a plan in place, and my thoughts razor-focused.

And I know just how to clear my head.

Turning, I head toward Charlotte's room.

I open the door to find the room empty, everything in its place. For a moment, I stop, fear trickling down my spine. Did she hear? Is she in the closet packing at this very moment? Something feral replaces the fear.

At this point, I'm not sure what I would do to keep her, but I know I'd go pretty fucking far.

Is this going to abate when I've finally claimed her? That's what Jake, Luke, and Roman seem to think, but I'm not so certain.

This doesn't feel like the sort of thing that's going away...

I cross to the bathroom, trying the knob, but it's locked. I should have made a key because I hate being locked out. I need to touch her, know that we're all good, that she didn't hear those words Leo said.

Charlotte has no idea how well I know her. There are so many messed up problems between us that it maybe means I should quit. Instead, I'm using all that information to my advantage.

I know her mom left her, understand her dad died. She has one good friend now, because she retreated from all the others, and the only reason Kim is still in her life is because Kim is the sort of woman you can't shake without real effort.

And if Charlotte senses that I am using her, playing her... she'll either retreat or bolt. I know it.

Abandonment is her wound the way revenge is mine and it's the one place I cannot tread hard.

I'm not getting into the bathroom, not without breaking down the door. I knock, but don't get an answer and then I step back, contemplating if it's actually a good idea to give it a good hard kick.

Leo's got me frothing, part of me knows that. Which means I should take a breath and not go hard at this. I don't want to scare her...

So stepping back from the door, I circle the room instead. The vanity, which usually sits empty, is now decorated with items. And I do mean decorated. The artful arrangement of the items somehow makes the place homier and more beautiful.

Kim's picture and a few others rest on the two nightstands, and she's added a colorful throw to the bed that she must have packed from her apartment. It's nice…

I pass by the bed and into the closet where I can hear the shower running in the bathroom.

The clothes that I bought for her and the ones she brought are arranged in neat rows on the custom shelves, not a thing out of place.

I also happen to know she didn't used to be this way. She's always been neat, but she wasn't so obsessive about the arrangement of items. But after her dad…

I'm a man who does his homework, and at some point, I managed to catch one of her former roommates in a bar. The coed was beyond chatty and within minutes I had a whole history.

Charlotte had withdrawn from all her friends, her inability to tolerate the mess of roommates drove her to live in that shitty apartment where she could be on her own. The other girls were pissed about it. She'd left them without a fourth or some shit.

I've seen this side of Charlotte in action. She can't tolerate anything out of place. Not even my kitchen.

When my dad was killed by Giovani Vendetti, I retreated into my family. Their livelihood and protection became my whole existence.

That and revenge. It doesn't even matter that Vendetti had cause, the way that man murdered my father will be avenged.

But Charlotte went a different route in her grief, she pulled away from everyone. My girl needs some love.

The implication of the word *love* isn't lost on me. But I don't mean it like I'm in love. Just that she needs someone looking out for her. Care and attention.

I hear the shower turn off and I leave the closet, and go sit on the bed. It takes her ten minutes in the bathroom and I apply myself to not fidgeting because that's not my style.

I'm a man of patience and determination. I don't get uppity like a fucking schoolboy. But between fighting with Leo and the tension that's been building with Charlotte, I can barely sit still.

She comes out wrapped in a towel, starting when she sees me.

I swear the towel shows less than most of the dresses I bought her but the knowledge that with a small tug she'd be naked in front of me has my cock stiffening in my slacks.

Her hair is wet, her face free of makeup and she looks like she's been crying. That has me standing.

"What's wrong, baby?" The words are out of my mouth before I've even gathered her in my arms, but she's stiff in my embrace.

"I should go. I shouldn't be here."

I stiffen, my hands tightening on her towel. I know she's saying this because of Leo. Did she hear what he said? Is she about to bolt? That's Charlotte's M.O. too. Leave when things get tough. Let her try and go. She'll find I'm a very hard man to shake.

CHAPTER THIRTEEN

Charlotte

Tension is rolling off Mason in waves. I feel it, his arms like iron bands about me. "Go where?"

"I don't know," I whisper, already knowing I'm saying ridiculous things. "I've been saving to leave Las Vegas once I got my degree. I could just disappear. Go back to Nebraska. Head to my aunt in Canada."

"You've been planning to leave Vegas?"

I nip at my lip. "I am graduating. It's natural to..." But my voice tapers off at the ferocity of his stare.

"What are you running from that scares you in Vegas?"

I swallow down a lump. "I thought I was best out of sight, out of mind."

He's got me tight against his front, and even through the towel, I can feel the hard press of his cock against my belly. "You were going to run from me."

"You did threaten me." My voice is small. Because after two years, it was pretty clear he wasn't going to hurt me. But it's just...things felt complicated here and...

He leans down, pressing his lips to the base of my throat where my pulse is thrumming wildly. "And you do like to run."

What's he talking about? But his teeth are nipping at my skin, causing a riot of sensations, even as the fingers of one his hands trace the top of the towel. "I haven't run anywhere."

"And you're not going to now."

I slowly shake my head. Because even though I have doubts about Mason, I know for right now, I'm safest with him. "No, I'm not."

He relaxes a bit. "Did Leo scare you, sweetheart?"

I shake my head again. "Only a little. But I know you won't let him hurt me."

"Never," he whispers into my neck as he finds the fold of the towel where one end is tucked to secure it and gives it a hard tug, sending the damp cloth to the floor.

I gasp, but he's crushing me to his chest again, the hand that had been clenched on the towel at the small of my back, now cupping my ass, his fingers squeezing into my softness.

It's commanding and a bit rough, but also...delicious. My head arches back and he skates his mouth down to the tip of one rosy breast, my skin still pink from my shower.

He sucks the nipple into his mouth, his tongue swirling about the puckering flesh as his teeth playfully bite. Maybe it's a little harder than playful, but I cry out in pleasure, the little spike of pain making it even better.

He lets go of my ass cheek, but it's only to slide his hand between my legs, cupping my sex in his palm.

I cry out but there is no pain in this touch. It's all pleasure and I throb with need at the pressure he's applying.

Instead of giving more, though, he eases his fingers out from between my legs. I let out a mewling protest, so tired of him bringing me closer and closer and then withdrawing again.

I'm way over my head here, because his control, the very thing I take great comfort in, is also his greatest weapon in positioning me however he wants. And I'm ready to do nearly anything to convince him to take me all the way.

This is how Mason wins. Always.

He gives me a devilish one-sided grin as he tugs off his shirt, revealing the chest that always makes me drool.

"Get on the bed, sweetheart."

For a moment, I'm frozen. This is it…I'm completely naked in front of him, he's kicking off his shoes as he gives me a look that tells me there is no room for argument.

His expression, one of domineering command, has me scrambling to do as he's asked. Whatever it is, I know I'm going to love it.

I take the two steps to the bed, stripping the covers back with one hand, before I start to climb in.

But I'm mid-way through the pivot, my hands on the mattress, one knee down on the mattress before I flip over, when a hand at my hip stops me.

"Both knees on the bed," he growls behind me. It's not a question, not even a request.

I do as he bids, now I'm on my hands and knees, the silk of the sheets brushing my palms, as his hand skims from my hips to trace the indent of my waist. He keeps going up my rib cage, his pinky brushing along my breast before he traces my shoulder and wraps his hand in my hair.

And then he gives a soft pull, arching my neck back and causing me to stick my behind further in the air.

"That's my good girl," he rumbles as he brings his other hand between my legs again.

He starts with the mound, his fingers pressing into the soft skin and hair, an ache pulsing through me because it feels so good, but also he's close to making me feel even better. I try not to squirm to move his fingers where I'm dying for his touch.

I must be dripping wet by now, a fact that's confirmed as he slides his middle finger over my clit.

I can't hold back my gasping moan, my body taking over and pushing into his hand, seeking more of the pleasure he's giving.

He pulls my hair harder, forcing me to still.

And then he begins a leisurely exploration of my folds, tracing my entrance with his fingers, continuing along my seam, past my vagina, to my anus. I've never dreamed anyone would touch me there, I tense as he circles it with his thumb. I can't deny that even that feels amazing. "I will conquer all of you, Charlotte," he murmurs, bending close. "But not all in one day."

And then he slides his hand back down, inserting a finger inside me, the walls of my vagina tightening around him.

It feels so good, being full of him that I cry out, clenching around him.

"No cumming yet," he pushes through gritted teeth. "You haven't said the magic word."

My eyes are squeezed shut and I have to force myself to open them and look back over my shoulder. "Ma...magic word?"

"What did I tell you, you were going to have to do?" He takes his finger back out, slowly rubbing up and down my seam, giving my clit a little tweak on the way.

It's so good and my breath catches on the smallest sob. "Please," I beg. "Please, Mason." I want him to make me cum. I want more of his skin on my skin. I just want...

"Please what..."

"Please make me cum, Mason."

"Are you begging me?"

Another little sob escapes my lips as I try to press deeper into his hand, but he pulls away again, leaving me empty. "I'm begging, Mason. Please."

"Good girl," he says, sounding like the predator he is. I nearly go limp with relief that he's going to finally give me what I've been craving.

But there's a pause as his hand slips from my hair. I look back in time to watch him drop to his knees behind me.

And then his tongue makes the same long pass that his fingers had made before. When he swirls his tongue over my clit, I begin to tremble it feels so good. But he doesn't keep the pressure there.

Instead, he keeps sliding his tongue from front to back, teasing every part of me until my body is a mass of bundled nerves so ready to break apart. I'm going to start begging again.

But I can't even form words. Broken little sounds tumble from my lips, half formed pleas that are moaned, my fingers twisting into the sheets.

And that's when he slides a thumb inside me, the rest of his hand nestling into the crack of my ass as he sucks my clit between his lips.

I scream, the pleasure so good and so intense, I break apart, an orgasm ripping through me.

He doesn't ease up until I've collapsed on the bed a trembling mess. It was so good, I don't even have words.

That's when I hear his zipper.

My face has sunk into the mattress, but my ass is still in the air, being held up by one of his hands.

I lift my head up just high enough to look over my shoulder. For the first time since I stepped out of the bathroom, fear skates down my spine.

Because my ass is in the air and his cock is out and...

The thick length of him is so much more than I bargained for.

He gives me another wicked smile. "Nervous, sweetheart?"

Lying is not really my thing. Not even small lies. So, I nod. "A little."

His hips ease forward but he doesn't push inside me. Instead, his cock glides along the crack of my ass. "We can't have that."

I can see the engorged head as his balls slap against my sensitive clit and I gasp and shudder, a sweet pain zinging through me.

"Do you want to cum again, baby?"

He slides away and then repeats the thrust, using my ass crack to... I don't know how to describe it...but it's almost like he's masturbating. There's no penetration.

I relax again, no longer worried. "Yes, please," I moan, my face sinking back against the mattress.

Without warning, he flips me over, the move only taking a single arm. Maybe I should be scared.

This man has me begging under him, his strength and control so superior to my own. But I can't help myself. Instead of being scared, the move only makes me hotter.

He leans over me, holding one of my breasts in each hand as he sucks one nipple and then the other.

I can feel the need building in me again as I thread my hands into his hair.

The head of his cock pushes against my clit, making me squirm against him, seeking more friction. I want him closer, so I hook one of my legs around his.

Was I frightened a minute ago? As he effortlessly brings my body to a frenzy once again, all I can think is how I want to belong to this man completely.

But he doesn't yield to the pressure of my leg, instead, he lifts up, grabs his cock at the base with his hand and swirling the head along my clit.

My hips are flexing to chase the pleasure and I'm giving little cries of protest… I want more. His hand slides back up my body, wrapping around the back of my neck, his fingers burrowing into my hair.

"Patience, sweetheart."

"I want—"

"I know what you want, trust me to give it to you." And then he leans down, capturing my mouth with his.

The kiss is full of the passion that's simmering just under the surface, his tongue plundering my mouth.

When he lifts up, his eyes are dark and stormy. "I'm not taking your virginity today."

I protest, pushing up on my elbows. "You promised that when I begged, you'd take it from me." I don't even recognize myself. I was scared a moment ago. I'm the one who made it to twenty-two without having sex at all. But Mason has me pleading with him to take my virginity. How did that happen?

He starts stroking himself, his other hand flexing to arch my neck more. "We're not in a rush. We only get to have the first time once.

Trust me when I say that delaying this a bit longer will only make it better."

Damn this man and his iron control.

His hand presses to my mound, his thumb stroking over my clit. "I shouldn't make you cum again for questioning me like that."

My eyes go wide because the way he's touching me now, I need to cum again…it feels like I need another orgasm the way I need air.

Mason has always been gentle. I like gentle. But that doesn't mean he's a man to be questioned.

For a moment I look up at him, wondering how I make sure I get what I need.

Arching my neck further, my chest sticks out as I spread my legs a bit wider. "Please, Mason. I'll be such a good girl. Please make me cum."

CHAPTER FOURTEEN

Mason

Fuck me. I've always found this girl irresistible. I've been dreaming of this moment for actual years, and the reality… It's better.

Spread out and arched, those pretty lips have done the sweetest begging. I want to sink into her so bad, my balls are like fucking rocks, they're clenched so tight and cum is tingling through my cock waiting to explode out.

But I'm going to wait.

Because one, she's a little scared still. I saw it when she first locked eyes on my cock. I like to dominate, there is no denying that. But I want a woman who is getting as much pleasure from that as I am.

And Charlotte doesn't just like my brand of sex. She loves it.

But she's so new at this, it would be ridiculously easy to frighten her off. And so I'm going to treat her with care as I slowly lead her where I want us to go.

Cum starts to leak out the tip, dripping on her belly but she's asked so nicely, that I force myself to wait, pushing her further up the bed so I can lock my mouth on her clit again. This one doesn't tease. With brutal precision, I suck on her with enough force that she's already shaking, her cries filling the room as she scratches at my shoulders, drawing blood. It only fuels me on, and I've got two fingers inside her, pushing on that spot deep in her that I know will break her wide open.

As much as I'm in a rush, I slow long enough to watch her face as she screams my name, the orgasm ripping through her.

It's the last shred of my control and I rear up, my cock in my hand, and with a few good pumps, I'm squirting cum all over her belly.

I squeeze my eyes shut a couple times because they're blurring and I want to see this crystal clear.

The sight of my cum on her body is like laying claim and it might be the sexiest thing I've ever seen or done.

Until she runs her finger through it, spreading a line of it into her skin and then she brings her fingertip to her lips.

Tongue out, she licks the tip of her finger before she sucks it clean.

My cock is rock hard again in a second. It's like I never even came. But her eyes are fluttering closed now, her arm settling above her head.

I know I'm going to need her again soon. But it can wait. For now, my girl needs some rest, and her care comes before anything else. "Where's your ring, sweetheart?"

Her eyes flutter open, meeting mine. The soft grey depths hold me captive for a moment. "Jewelry holder. Bathroom."

"A place for everything," I say, pushing off the side of the bed and entering the bathroom. Grabbing a washcloth, I wet it with warm water before I pluck the diamond from the velvet folds of the holder.

Heading back out to the bedroom, she's already asleep exactly where I left her. A satisfied smile curls my lips. I wore her out.

I slip the ring on her finger, her eyes fluttering open once again.

I told her that the engagement was part of the protection plan, and it is. But I like seeing the ring on her finger. It's another claim that isn't just for me. Any man will see it and know…

I take the cloth, and gently clean her up. "I've got a big soaking tub," I say as I cast the cloth aside. "Tomorrow, you are taking a bath."

"Mmm," she murmurs as she curls onto her side.

I slip into the bed, pulling the covers up over us both, nestling her back against my front.

Her skin slides against mine like silk and lace as I wrap my arm around her. She's already fallen back to sleep and I kiss the top of her head, closing my eyes too. I don't think I'm going to sleep, not after everything that's happened tonight, but she's warm and soft. Settling her even closer, I slip off to sleep within seconds.

I don't wake until the sun is rising, unusual for me, but when I do, Charlotte is still nestled against my body, her scent wrapped about me.

I bend down a bit, kissing her head, the scratches on my shoulders pulling as she stirs against me. "Good morning," she murmurs in this sultry sleepy voice.

"Good morning," I answer a small smile tugging at my lips. I don't do sleepovers. Then again, I've never let a woman move in, either.

Charlotte is a lot of firsts for me too.

I skim my fingers down her arm and then under the covers, tracing the narrow curve of her waist and the flare of her hips.

She feels so good, I'm hard enough to cut glass before I'm even sinking my fingers into her slick folds.

She moans, her legs parting for me, and I let out a satisfied growl as I start massaging my fingers through her pussy.

She gives the slightest wince, and I ease back, knowing she's sore. But if the goal was to dump enough cum to think straight before my meeting this morning, I'm not even close.

If anything, the buzzing in my brain has only intensified. I want to touch her, explore her, mark her with my cum.

I keep my touch light and easy, slowly working her back to the point where she's not wincing but panting.

This time, I want more than a jerk though, so kneeling next to her, I toss the covers back, and roll her onto her back and, parting her legs, bury my face between her thighs.

She tastes so fucking good. Not something you tell a woman, but she's going to have trouble keeping my mouth from her pussy. I could eat her all day.

I run my tongue from tip to tip, cum already boiling in my balls thinking of being inside that sweet pussy.

But I'm totally distracted when her soft, small hand wraps around my cock. I growl out my satisfaction, lifting up to see her fingers wrapped about me, the pale skin of her hand in sharp contrast to my raging erection.

It's gorgeous, and sometime in the not-too-distant future, I will let her touch me like this for as long as she wants.

But right now, much as I am the man who waxed poetic about delaying gratification, I need some.

And I'm looking for more than her soft little hand…fantastic as it is.

Which is why I swing one of my knees to the other side of her ribs. Bending down, I lap her clit again, the position naturally dangling my cock right in her face.

Charlotte takes the hint and her tongue darts out to lick the pearl of cum that has collected on tip.

"Fuck," I rumble into her skin, my eyes closing. Her scent is all around me as her lips start nibbling at my cock.

Suddenly more impatient than I've been for anything in a very long time, I push past her lips, the engorged head sinking into her mouth.

It feels so good that I keep going, Charlotte's mouth opening for me to accommodate my girth as my cock slides along her tongue.

She takes me in with only a slight choke and I pull back out, a small graze of her teeth just making it better as I dive back into my breakfast. I eat her like a starving man and soon I'm pumping in and out of her mouth as I work three fingers into her tight pussy.

Charlotte's going to have to build up to my cock and this is the best way I can think of to help her prepare.

If it hurts, she doesn't show any signs, her hips moving to the frantic rhythm I've set, her moans of pleasure muffled by my erection pumping in and out of her mouth. It's fast and messy and so fucking fantastic. When she starts to squeeze my fingers, her thighs tremble and I'm on the edge of cumming too.

The fire raging inside me is unlike any other I've ever felt, and I know in this moment, I'm not fucking her out of my system.

The more I get, the more I'm going to want.

She explodes underneath me and it's my cue to let go, the orgasm tearing a roar from my throat as I pump into her mouth, her fingers digging into my hips, pulling me closer.

But I pull out, spinning around and gathering her against my chest before she's even finished the tremors of her own orgasm.

I bury my hand in her hair. "Charlotte," I say, rough and raw as I gather her closer. "Sweetheart."

One of her arms wraps about my shoulders, her fingers skimming down my back. "Oh wow," she breathes in my ear. "I'm not sure how I'm even going to walk today."

That pulls a rough laugh from my lips, as I hold her even tighter. Does she have any idea what those words do to me? Does she want to bind me tighter to her? It's working. "So don't."

She leans back and gives me a lazy smile. "A day in bed? Are you staying with me?"

I frown, my body stiffening, and I know she feels it. That slight withdrawal. I have my family today. Business. And then there's Leo and the fight we just had.

"I wish I could, sweetheart. But I've got…" I taper off thinking about the meeting I scheduled this morning. Leo and I are about to face off again. The problems are coming in from all sides and I'm going to need all my wits to make it through this mountain of problems.

So why do I just want to stay in bed with Charlotte? Since my father died, it's been all fight and nothing soft. No sweetness.

Then again, do I even deserve sweet? More specifically, do I deserve Charlotte?

"I know," she sighs. "I'll just miss you, that's all."

"I'll miss you too," I answer, meaning the words. I get up from the bed, cradling her in my arms and carry her toward the door.

"Where are we going?" she asks, her arms wrapping about my neck.

"The bath. Remember? We've got to make certain we're taking good care of you. Because when I get home tonight…"

The waiting is nearly over. Charlotte is about to be fully and completely mine. It's a dangerous emotion, but I'm starting to feel as though I would be willing to burn down the world to keep her.

The problem…that's exactly how my father ended up dead in a gutter.

CHAPTER FIFTEEN

CHARLOTTE

I LOUNGE BACK AGAINST MASON, the giant tub easily holding us both. The warm water had been filled with Epsom salt and it is doing wonders to soothe my sore skin.

Mason washes my arms, my legs, my stomach, his hands stroking over my skin, but he'd been careful to keep his touches sweet and not sexual.

That didn't stop me from feeling his erection pressed into my behind.

I reach back to skate my fingers along the engorged skin, but he stops me. "You need a break and I need to get to work."

I sigh out my disappointment as he kisses me and then rises up from the bath, stepping out and into the shower as I watch from the tub, the sight of his hands skimming over his own skin, sending my pulse racing once again. The man is a god. I rest my face on the cool tile of the tub's edge, wishing we could hide from the world and stay wrapped in this cocoon for a little while longer. Even if it's mostly fiction, it's been wonderful.

Mason turns off the shower, opening the glass door and wrapping a towel low on his hips, his chest and abs still on full display. I can't get enough of looking at this man. Leaning over the tub, he kisses me again, my lips clinging to his as I close my eyes.

"Cold yet?" his fingers gently brush over my cheek.

"Almost."

He reaches for my hand, clasping my fingers in his and then pulls me out, stepping back into his shower and turning it on.

A wave of emotion rises up in my chest as he closes the shower door, leaving me to my shower. I could get used to being cared for. How long had it been?

Dipping my head under the hot spray, I wash up and then wrap in a towel, heading out of Mason's room and into my own.

As I step out into the hall, he calls from the kitchen. "I'll be back tonight. Breakfast is already out."

I pivot, stepping into the living room. "Bye." The word comes out tight. Last night and this morning had been like a dream, and they'd left me feeling...vulnerable. Emotional.

Does he do this with all the women he's dated? Because I'd made that comment about playing house...but this didn't feel like play. It feels real and it's messing with my head.

Our engagement is fake. It's for my protection and his...enjoyment? That doesn't feel quite right. I look down at the diamond sparkling on my finger, wondering if it holds any answers.

He comes to my side, giving me one more long kiss before he's gone. I can't see the elevator from here, the hallway blocking the doors, but I can hear it close, the soft whir of it carrying Mason down to the parking garage.

My head dips as I turn to my room, facing another day of being alone with little to do.

I take my time getting ready, testing all my new makeup and products, carefully blowing out my hair.

I look at the effect in my bathroom mirror, turning my head. I look like a billionaire's fiancé, styled like this.

Going into my closet, I pick out a dress, and then put on my jewelry. One hour down, many more to go…

Grabbing my laptop, I decide to look through my pictures, check my email, and send a message to Kim. It's been way too long since I reached out and she must be worried. We're talk-every-day kind of friends.

But as I open my account, the first email that catches my attention is sent from UNLV. My heart leaps into my throat.

With a trembling hand, I click open the email to find my worst nightmare come to life. In completely plain terms, the email states that the university would allow me to walk during graduation, but if I wished to receive my degree, I'd have to repeat my visual arts class. It's a requirement for the degree and my grade is failing.

My vision blurs as my hand comes to my mouth. I have so few things I really want to complete in my life…

I probably would have left Vegas after what had happened with the Kincaids two years ago. I've been fighting the urge to flee, but I'd held back because this was more important.

Mason alluded to the fact that I was a runner last night, and I'm not sure he's wrong. After my mom left, I convinced my dad to move to a new town. I didn't want to be known as the girl whose mom didn't love her enough to stay.

In high school, I'd quit track when my coach pressed me to be tougher. I was a hard worker, but he seemed like the type who'd never be pleased. And after my dad's death, it had taken everything in me not to leave Vegas. My degree had been the only thing holding me here.

And now…it's slipping through my fingers.

Pushing up, I slam the laptop closed and begin to pace back and forth in my room. I pick up the phone Mason gave me, intent upon calling him, but then I drop it again.

He's fighting with Leo, running a business, trying to neutralize a threat that already exists in my life.

How many problems can I drop at his door?

And as nice as it feels to have him take care of me, I did live life on my own for actual years. Besides, I ought to be careful not to take advantage of his strength. This is already short term, there is nothing like a needy woman to make a short-term thing shorter. While I don't date, I've watched my roommates go through countless men and nothing ends a relationship faster than clingy or needy.

I look at the clock, noting that Professor Burke's office hours start in fifteen minutes.

Drawing in a deep breath, I lift the phone up again, choosing the other number that's been programmed in.

"Jackson?" I ask when someone picks up.

"It's me," Mason's driver answers. "Did you need something?"

"A ride to UNLV."

There is a pause. "A ride? For what?"

I nip at my lip. "Just something I need to finish up for the semester." It's the truth.

He pauses again, the line silent for several seconds before he seems to finally make a decision. "Come on down."

Letting out a long breath of air, I step into the closet, picking out a pair of low-heel sandals before I head for the elevator.

During the ride down, I prepare what I'm going to say to Professor Burke. I'm not much for threatening or bluffing. But I know I did excellent work on that project. Do I take this to other administrators?

I could use Mason's name, but if Mason is trying to pass me off as his long-term girlfriend turned fiancé and not the waitressing college student, that seems unwise.

I have another niggle of doubt as I step out of the elevator. Does this impact Mason's plan? Should I wait for him?

What if he tells me that in the grand scheme of problems, failing a class falls into the worry-about-that-problem-later category? That it's not important.

I don't want to worry later. This is the entire reason I'm still here, and to me, this might be more important than any of them. Graduating is a do-before-I-die kind of item.

With that in mind, I square my shoulders as the doors open and I step out into the garage.

Vegas is already heating up for the day, the warmth of the late morning making me instantly sticky. But the car is running, the air conditioning on, as Jackson opens the rear door for me, his kind smile firmly in place.

I slide into the cool car, trying to come up with a plan. I'll tell the truth. My work this semester has been worthy of passing the class. If he doesn't give me the grade I deserve, I'll tell everyone about his proposition, present my work, and ask him to justify my suddenly failing grades. It's the best I've got.

Wiping my palms on my dress, I try to keep my breathing even, but my hands clench and unclench in my lap as the car pulls out of the lot.

"Everything all right?" Jackson asks, his eyes meeting mine in the rearview.

"Trouble with one of my classes," I answer, staring out the window as I mentally rehearse again. "I'm going to get it straightened out."

"Not Professor Burke?"

"What?" That pulls me from my thoughts, my brow crinkling. Had I mentioned my professor's name?

"You let me know if you need any help," he says. "I don't look it now, but I used to be pretty tough."

I smile, relaxing into my seat. "Thank you, Jackson. That really does make me feel better."

He gives a nod and then silence falls between us while he navigates Vegas traffic. It takes less than fifteen minutes before he turns the car onto the campus, parking near the Building of the Arts.

I step out of the car, taking one last fortifying breath as Jackson falls into step next to me, typing on his phone.

"You don't have to come inside with me," I start, but he doesn't even look up.

Instead, he keeps typing. "I definitely do. Mason would have my hide if I let you out of my sight."

I wince, wondering once again if this is a mistake. Maybe I should have spoken with Mason first. But I'm here now and I'm going to use my newfound confidence to try and solve this problem myself.

Making my way inside, the cool halls have that familiar smell that calms my nerves. I loved this place until this semester. It's been my home and I draw some strength from that.

I round the corner for Professor Burke's office, the door is closed. I can just hear voices coming from inside. He's likely meeting with another student.

I wait for nearly ten minutes, fidgeting as Jackson stands stoically next to me, periodically checking his phone. A woman my age finally exits the small room, her eyes welling with tears. Am I not the only one Burke is manipulating?

I give her a sympathetic look before I turn toward the open door, drawing a deep breath, and knocking. "Professor Burke?"

His gaze lifts to mine. It's obvious that Burke used to be a handsome man. He still has nice eyes, a warm smile. But his hair is thinning as his waistline has expanded. It's not a big deal, everyone gets older but the fact that he's still trying to sleep with women in their early twenties is just creepy.

"Close the door, Charlotte."

I do as he commands, drawing in a deep breath through my nose to calm my nerves before I turn back to him.

He looks me up and down, his lip curling with a bit of disdain. "Glammed up, I see."

I touch my hair, that feeling that I've made a mistake hitting me in the chest again. I look like Mason's fiancé today, not like my college student self. I should have put my hair in a scrubby ponytail, worn my old clothes.

Burke has noticed the change and alarm bells are already pinging in my head. If Mason were confronting someone, he would have considered every detail. I've barely begun, and I already feel like a fool.

"I want to talk to you about my failing grade."

"What about it?"

"I deserve to pass your class."

He sneers at me, leaning over his desk. "That's the thing about being the student, Charlotte. You don't get to pick your grades."

"I completed the assignments, meeting all criteria, and turned them in on time."

"Says you."

"You're right. I do say. In fact, I have a lot of things to say," I answer back, my voice dropping like Mason's does when he's mad. One of the many things that man does exceptionally well. He intimidates with his voice alone.

Burke stands and starts coming around his desk. "Like what?"

"I wonder what the department chair will think when I present the work and the dates," I say, my fists clenching. I refuse to take a step back. "I wonder what she'll think when she hears about your proposition—" But I don't get any more words out before his hand wraps around my arm like a band of steel.

He's going to leave bruises, I think, as he tugs me forward, pinning me between himself and the desk.

I cry out, turning my head to the side, as he leans close, his hot mouth comes to my cheek. "You know what, Charlotte. You're right. I've been hasty. I'm going to pass you. But first..." And then he leans back, just long enough to spin me around so that my back is to his front. It only takes a second, and I'm disoriented, as he pins me to the desk again, the hard wood of his desktop pressing into the front of my legs.

I try to fight, but my hands lash out uselessly. I had maybe a second to escape, a moment that I missed, and now I'm trapped and weaker than him.

Grabbing the back of my head, he pushes my torso down on his desk. I finally grab his wrist and dig my nails in to loosen his grip, but he's too strong.

He's yanking at my hair and I'm clawing and scratching, my cry surely alerting someone. Jackson is out there. If I could just...

That's the moment the door bursts open. I try to lift my head, a chest comes into view but it doesn't belong to Jackson.

Instead, Mason fills the opening. Burke startles, partially releasing me and I lift my chin to meet Mason's gaze. He stares back, his cold rage written on every line of his face. I gasp to see him, my eyes wide.

With a snarl, he closes the distance between us. Then he rears his hand back to box Professor Burke across the ear.

I suppress a wild giggle, half born of fear and half relief that Mason smacked my professor like an errant child.

Burke goes crashing to the side and just like that, I'm free. I stand spinning, my breath gasping from my lungs, but Mason has not stopped in front of me.

Instead, he's standing over Professor Burke. Grabbing him by the arm, he picks him up like he's a rag doll, even though Professor Burke is a full-grown man and a somewhat heavy one at that.

For Professor Burke's part, the fear that had surely lit my eyes a few moments ago now fills his…

My hands clasp over my mouth, as I watch the turn of events unfold. It's almost odd that my professor, who dominated me just moments ago, is now at Mason's mercy.

Mason drops his face to Professor Burkes, his voice deadly calm. "Do you want to explain to me why you had your hands on my wife?"

The word wife slices through me. And apparently it does Professor Burke too. "Wife? I didn't know. I thought…"

"You thought she was alone and that you could take advantage." Mason shakes him with every word, and I swear I hear Burke's teeth rattle. "Jackson," Mason calls. "Did you see what happened?"

"I saw it all," Jackson replies from the doorway, but I don't look at him. I'm completely focused on Mason.

His lip curls. "That's a shame for you, professor. Witnesses are messy for naughty teachers who could lose their positions."

Burke goes completely pale.

"Obviously, my wife is going to pass your class."

"Y-y-yes," Burke answers as quickly as he can get the word out.

"The question is…" Mason's voice has taken on that tone I remember from years ago. The same one I'd gotten that first night in the conference room. Cold. Deadly. "Which form of punishment do you prefer?"

"Punishment…" Burke croaks.

"We can go through the proper channels," Mason's voice has

dropped just above a whisper. "Where I have you fired, stripped of your position, and banned from teaching anywhere ever again. Or…" Mason's face is only an inch from Burke's. "You can take your beating like a man."

The smell of urine fills the office and I know Professor Burke has pissed himself. My nose wrinkles.

"Wait out in the hall, sweetheart," Mason says to me, speaking to me for the first time since he barged into the room. "Better yet, take her to my car, Jackson."

I don't argue as I leave the office, allowing Jackson to escort me down the hall. But even through the closed door, I hear a crack followed by the sound of a grown man crying.

A moment's satisfaction pulses through me, until I realize…I'm not without guilt today either.

Mason is surely going to punish me too.

CHAPTER SIXTEEN

MASON

SMACKING around the professor has done little to calm the hectic feeling inside me that settled in my chest the moment I opened that door.

The sight of another man touching Charlotte like that…I want to rip something apart. Tear it to pieces and then light it on fire.

No one gets to touch her like that. Not even me. I don't mean playful hair pulling or a good romp doggy style. That fucking asshole meant to hurt and humiliate her.

Of course, I paid that back in spades. And if Burke steps a toe out of line, I'll burn that motherfucker to the ground.

But now I have to deal with my errant woman, and I am not happy.

I'd called her wife in there. I'd meant it to further worry Burke. Men understand this universal rule…you do not mess with a woman who's been fully claimed by another. The strange part was that the word had tasted good on my tongue. Right.

I reach the parking lot and yank open the limo door to find Charlotte sitting quietly to one side, her hands folded, her gaze on her lap.

To see her quiet actually soothes some of my ruffled feathers, but not all of them. She's not so hurt that she's hysterical. Then again, she was exceptionally calm that first night in the conference room. Doesn't she have any sense for her own safety? "What were you thinking?" I snarl, slamming the door behind me. "He could have really hurt you."

Her head tilts up, her eyes, shining with tears, meet mine. "I'm sorry," she whispers. "I didn't think."

"No. You didn't."

"I just wanted to fix one problem without adding more worries to your already full plate. I'm so sorry..."

She's talking about me? If she'd argued, I could have stayed mad. But her apology cuts me to shreds and I'm pulling her into my lap, my arms wrapping tight around her. "I won't even go into the fact that our entire ruse could be jeopardized. What if someone looking for you saw you on that campus and made the connection?"

She stiffens in my arms, her breath catching. "I didn't see anyone other than one female student who I don't know."

"Still. It was dangerous." I hold her tighter, my bruised knuckles aching as I twist my fists into her dress.

"It's time for me to go, isn't it?"

My arms turn to steel around her. She's getting antsy to run again. "No. It's time for you to let me take care of this."

"It's too much. I've asked too much. I can't ask you to do that."

Reaching for her chin, I tilt up her face to mine, claiming her mouth in a fierce kiss. After what she just went through, I should be tender. But my blood is still pumping, and the worry is still beating through my veins. I let her mouth go, giving her a long stare so that she understands. "Charlotte, I am big enough and strong enough to hold up your world. Just let me."

She melts into me then, her body pressing close to mine, her mouth so soft and yielding that I could devour her. God, this woman feels so good.

She threads her fingers into my hair, her full lips opening. I kiss her over and over, wishing that I could go home with her. Just spend the afternoon washing all her hurts away and hold her until she fell asleep in my arms.

What is this woman doing to me?

But I had a meeting with my family that had started a half hour ago, and they were going to be pissed. I'd been about to go to the conference room when I'd seen Jackson's text that Charlotte had requested to go to the campus.

By the time I read it though, they were already en route. I'd left without a word to anyone, rushing to follow her.

Which meant I was now very late. Kincaids were not known for patience.

As if the situation wasn't already tense enough. Which is why I hold Charlotte until we reach the apartment and then I see her into the elevator myself.

It's only when the doors close, that I put my war face back on.

My knuckles are red and bloody from where I've pummeled Burke's face, but I don't mind the pain.

If anything, it puts me in the right state of mind.

This is a battle, and I'm going to need my fight. I get out at Kincaid Enterprises and make my way up the elevator and into the conference room. The doors have barely opened, and I can already feel the change of energy.

Everyone is tense and or pissed. Join the club.

Roman and Luke stand when I enter. Jake always keeps his seat and today is no exception. He might be my employee, but as my uncle, he doesn't bow.

Leo stands off to one side, his glare strong enough to shred me. I stop, our eyes locking.

"You look like fucking shit," Jake calls from his seat.

"I feel great," I respond back. Snark isn't usually my style, but it suits my mood today.

Roman shakes his head. "Why are your hands bleeding?"

Everyone stills at that…even Leo. "It's unrelated." For them, it is.

Luke's eyes narrow, as he assesses me with a long glare. "Can you really afford to fight with anyone else?"

He's not wrong. But if I tell them I was kicking Charlotte's professor's ass, they are going to get the wrong idea. Actually, they'll get the right idea. Charlotte matters to me when she shouldn't. I told them I'd sacrifice her for their benefit and yet here I am, righting every wrong in her life.

Which sounds an awful lot like a man who has fallen, and we've got a pact. It was business and family first, sex second, and love never.

Leo has scented my weakness though and he's stalking toward me, chest puffed. "Tell us anyway. We've been waiting for this story for forty-five minutes."

"Let's just get down to it," I say, moving to my chair.

They all watch me, and I know they all know. I'm not myself…and every single one of them is worried I'm slipping. Making the sort of mistakes that might detonate the business. Get one of us killed.

"This is business," Leo sneers. "See, I think that you're losing your grip and that what this operation needs is a change of leadership."

I push back out of my chair. "Now see, yesterday, when you showed up uninvited at my apartment, I told you the truth. You are the one who is thinking like a child and not considering the family or the business."

"And you're thinking with your fucking cock," Leo fires back. "Is she soft and warm, big brother? I bet her mouth looks so good wrapped around your dick. Those lips always were fucking amazing."

I'm over the table in a hot second, vaulting the four-foot-wide surface and tackling Leo because Charlotte's mouth should never be on his mind.

I take him to the ground, both of us rolling as I plant my fist in his face. He gets me good with a solid rib shot.

"Stop," Luke barks, both of us ignoring him as Leo swings hard, catching my jaw and sending my head snapping back. My face is going to hurt for days.

But I barely feel it now, going back in for more…

It's Luke who hauls me off, Roman jumping on Leo to keep him from the counterattack.

Jake is puffing on his cigar. "I guess you boys didn't learn from your father after all. Never let a woman get involved."

I shake off Luke, running a hand through my hair. The Italian mob offed my dad because of the giant debt he'd collected.

But a few people knew the whole story. He'd been fucking the Italian mafia's queen, Maria Carcetti, and when Toni Carcetti, her husband, had figured it out, he'd hired a hit on my father. We all knew pussy clouded judgment.

And everyone in this room already knew that mine was impaired.

I knew it too.

Leo shakes off Roman and charges toward me, only stopping when his finger is in my face. "This isn't over, Mason. You're not taking the ship down like he did. I won't let it happen."

He shoves me and then charges for the elevators.

"Then stay and fight," I snarl back. "And stop stomping off like a bitch."

He spins, charging at me and I drop my stance, getting ready, but Luke knocks him off kilter so that he crashes into the wall.

Roman stands in front of me. "Leo, you can't just declare yourself leader. It doesn't work like that."

Luke stands next to Roman. "We decide together. That's how it's always been."

"Fucking fine," Leo snarls. "You don't want me to be in charge. At least remove him..." He jabs his finger at me. "He's losing his touch."

Jake draws another puff from his cigar. "If you're asking for a vote, we'll vote."

"I am," Leo retorts. "And I need everyone to see the truth. Mason is going soft, and it will get us all killed."

"You are going off the deep end and that is the biggest danger we've got," I say, adding in my own two cents before the voting happens.

The room is silent as Leo and I lock gazes, neither looking away. We've both aired our grievances, there is no taking them back.

"All those in favor of removing Mason."

I pull my shoulders straighter. They want to take me out? We've been a unit this whole time because it insulates us from the mistakes my father made. That's the real reason we vote. No taking on larger amounts of debt to woo some woman. No making decisions with our egos.

But if they think they're taking the business I built away from me, they're sorely mistaken.

In that moment, I realize just how much Charlotte has distracted me because I did not anticipate this happening this quickly. And I always anticipate every move in the business sector. It wasn't that the signs weren't there. I've just been so focused on her…

Leo jabs his hand in the air. "Aye."

No one else speaks.

Slowly, Leo's lip curls as he stares from Kincaid to Kincaid. "Fine. That's the way you fuckers want it. That's the way you have it. But I'm not done here." With a snarl, he turns on heel and stalks to the elevator, jabbing the button and disappearing.

The breath slowly releases from my lungs. I've still got a chance to make this all right. I can beat the Italians, neutralize the Dukes, have our revenge on Toni Carcetti and Giovani Vendetti, and get the tunnel made to grow our business even bigger. It's a long list, with one more addition. Keep Charlotte safe.

"Well that sucked," Luke rumbles, looking at me. "You'd better keep it together Mason. Don't get us killed over a woman."

Charlotte. My chest tightens because I know, if it gets too hot…I'm going to have to let her go.

I don't mean today. I'll make certain she's safe. But she will have to go…this isn't permanent. It's part of our deal and falling in love isn't an option for me. Not ever.

She's messing with my life and my family in ways I promised I would never let happen.

CHAPTER SEVENTEEN

CHARLOTTE

I CHEW on one corner of my nail wondering if I can actually pull off what I'm about to do.

In the corner of my room, the nicest printer I've ever seen sits just outside its box. I don't know when Mason bought it for me, but I can guarantee it wasn't today.

I still can't believe what happened with Professor Burke today or how Mason materialized in the nick of time.

I touch up my makeup, looking down at the lingerie I'm wearing.

Mason had bought me several sets of sleepwear from demure to downright sexy and I've opted to use his T-shirts every other night I've been here, but not tonight.

Tonight, I've chosen a silky black number that hugs my curves, barely covering my rear end. The piece is sheer enough that I can just make out my nipples in my reflection in the vanity. The heart neckline is only held up by thin spaghetti straps. I've never worn anything like it in my life.

I've washed my hair and redried it, curling it into loose waves that I think look very sexy with the shorter length.

I've never played the game of seduction before, nor have I offered myself up for a punishment I actually know I earned, but I'm about to try for both...

I apply a bit of gloss to my lips when I hear the elevator door open. Pushing back from my stool, I try to decide where to stand. I wish I'd thought this part out. Do I greet him in the kitchen or wait here?

Maybe I should arrange myself on the bed. Or better yet...

"Charlotte."

Mason's low growl sounds dangerous tonight and I jump. "In here."

He's angry. Why wouldn't he be? Did I ruin everything or just his day?

I start to fidget. My mom left us, and I guess I always wondered why. My dad left too, not that he made the choice. But still.

Mason isn't staying in my life, I know that. All he ever claimed to want was my virginity, which he's very close to getting. Once he has it, does this all end? Or have I pushed him away before we can even get that far?

My door opens and I start toward it, trying to add a bit of sway to my hips. He stops when he sees me, his eyes darkening. "What's this?"

I draw in a breath. "I...I wanted to apologize."

"Accepted." He stares at me for another second, then two, his gaze unreadable. "I'm going to take a shower."

And then he's gone. My heart jumps into my throat as it tightens painfully. It's already happening. He's angry enough that he doesn't even care that I'm in lingerie.

Has the passion cooled that much already?

I start to follow, not sure if I'm actually allowed to enter his room. The only time I've been in it is when he invited me in this morning.

"Mason?" I call just as I hear the shower turn on.

He appears again, tugging at his tie and loosening his collar as I stand in his doorway. "What?"

"What's wrong?"

"I'm tired. It was a long damned day that involved not one, but two physical altercations."

I wince. "Leo?"

"Leo."

"You don't want me to make it better?" I nip at my lip as I slide my hands over my hips.

His eyes drift down me again. "Not right now."

This is bad. Really bad. "Is our agreement over?"

He pulls off his shirt and when the fabric clears his face, his gaze holds mine. Steady. Even. "Of course not. You think I'd let anyone hurt you?"

My breath blows out in a rush, a little relief making my shoulders drop down a notch. "But you're angry with me."

"I'm not." And then he starts to turn away.

I could cry out. I could chase him. Instead, I sink to my knees, parting my thighs as I do, so the black thong underwear I'm wearing is on clear display.

He stops in the doorway, going still, his eyes devouring me. I don't lean forward, don't lean closer. Instead, I lean back, resting on my hands, as I part my legs wider. I'm nervous…but even still, I can feel excitement stirring low in my belly.

Mason pivots back to face me, the intensity of his stare letting me know I've caught his attention.

"I know that I was bad today."

His shoulders draw up, his back going stiff and straight.

"You told Professor Burke that he needed to take his punishment for what he did."

"I should have ripped his throat out for what he tried to do to you." That has my attention. There is a ferocity in Mason's tone that is almost shocking. It doesn't frighten me, instead, I feel protected. Safe.

He crosses to where I am on the floor until he is standing over me. Reaching down, he skates his fingers over my jaw. "It's been a long day, sweetheart, and a traumatic one for you."

I can see his erection in his dress pants and my own body is aching with need. But I don't reach out and touch him. This is my punishment after all. But his touch, the fact that he's calling me sweetheart, has my chin lifting and my back arching up. His eyes skate down my body again.

"What is my punishment, Mason?" I want him to touch me and then I want him to make me cum and then I want to sleep in the circle of his very strong arms.

I'm not afraid of Mason, even after what happened with Burke today. Mason would never hurt me like that. But I'll feel safest of all with his heart beating against mine.

He crouches down then, resting on the balls of his feet, his elbows coming to his knees. He brings one hand to his jaw and his knuckles are a mess, even worse than this morning, I swear.

I gasp, wanting to touch them but I'm not doing anything I haven't been told so I hold still.

With his other hand, he reaches out and touches my bare knee, his fingers skimming up my thigh until he stops just before the thong.

I'm panting now, desperate for him to touch me more.

"Are you certain you're prepared to take your punishment today?"

My sex gives a throb of anticipation at his words. "Yes."

"Like I said, it's been a very long day."

I look into his dark brown eyes, so dark they appear almost black in this light. "I'm not afraid of your touch, Mason."

I've been afraid of Mason. I was scared of what he'd do to me, what he'd threatened. But even two years ago, when he'd carried me from that club, I'd held onto him like a lifeline. I've never been afraid of Mason's hands.

It's an interesting revelation as Mason stands, kicks off his shoes, takes off his belt, and sits on the edge of the bed.

"Come here, Charlotte."

I rise up from the floor, not scared, but not exactly rushing either. Am I going to like whatever he's about to do? Not?

I did ask for this, but now that the moment is here, my stomach gives a strange swoop, as I stop in front of him.

He reaches out with both hands to grasp my waist and then slides them over my hips, tracing my body. The touch is soothing, gentle, and I know in that moment, whatever we do, it will not be anger that motivates Mason. I further relax, wishing that I could press against him, wrap my arms around his neck and drop my cheek to the top of his head.

I want to touch him so much I ache, but I keep my hands at my sides. His grip tightens on my hips to one that is firm and then I'm tumbling into his lap, belly down, my head hanging over one side of his knee, my legs over the other, my rear in the air.

I know what he's going to do, but I'm not worried. In fact, I feel myself getting wetter.

He slides the thin fabric of my negligee up to my waist, the thong exposing both my cheeks. "Next time you have a problem, what are you going to do?"

"Talk to you," I whisper.

"And are you going to confront a man on your own again?"

"No."

He skims his fingers over the back of my thigh. "Good girl." And then he traces over the rounded flesh of my bare cheek. He lifts his hand and suddenly, his palm comes down with a hard stinging smack.

I jump, the spank unexpected, the pain reverberating through me. But with it, comes a pulsing pleasure, an ache between my legs that only intensifies as has hand comes down again, and then again.

I lose count. I think maybe ten. It doesn't matter because when he gives me the last smack, his hand immediately slides between my thighs, rubbing my seam through the cloth of my thong.

The pressure is so good, I cry out and the moment he presses against my clit, I start cumming.

But I barely finish the orgasm and he's flipping me over. I'm putty in his hands as he stands with me cradled in his arms, spinning around to lay me on his bed.

He bends over me and I twine my fingers into the waves of his hair, so glad to be touching him again. The thong is off, brushing down my legs as he moves down my body and my fingers slip from his hair.

But the moment he gets the underwear off my toes, he's climbing back up me, his shoulders parting my thighs as he grabs my hips and lifts me up to give me a long lick.

Panting, I give a low needy moan. It feels so good and the visual of his large hands grasping my hips and waist, his face between my legs is only making me hotter.

I reach for his hair again, pulling him closer but also just wanting to touch him.

I want this man to be mine. Always mine. My eyes close and my head falls back as I feel another orgasm building.

CHAPTER EIGHTEEN

MASON

I LOOK UP AT CHARLOTTE, her thighs trembling around my head, her hips arched to get more of my tongue, and I know that I am well and truly screwed.

I can't get enough of this woman. And with her under my roof, I'm not going to be able to hold myself away from her no matter the consequences.

Christ, I couldn't even last five minutes before I dove in face first. Literally.

I should send her to Roman or give Leo his way and...

I press harder on her clit, three fingers pumping in and out of her as she lets out a keening moan and I just know.

I'm not giving her up.

The very idea of another man touching her, protecting her, makes me insane. My free hand is spread over her belly, nearly covering the entirety of the surface, so that I can keep her from bucking away from my tongue. But I love how my hand looks slashed across her pale skin and I know I'm on the fast train to damnation.

My business is about to implode, my family rip apart, and what am I doing?

Eating Charlotte like a starving man.

Maybe the family was always going to tear. We are a family of alphas when there can be only one leader.

And possibly, the violence of so many criminal families in one place was always going to explode, detonating in a way that the damage could never be controlled.

But maybe, I'm a lot more like my old man than I thought possible. He couldn't see past good pussy, and neither can I.

Tomorrow I'll think about what that means. Right now, all I care about is watching Charlotte break apart on my tongue, and then having those gorgeous lips wrapped around my cock.

I should care. About my brothers, my family. I swore I would never put them through what our father did to us, but I've been fighting my feelings for Charlotte for a really long time and now that she's here in my house, in my bed…

I'm not sure how much more I can fight.

She's so close now, her face twisted up, her fingers digging into my scalp. I stop caring about tomorrow as I suck her clit hard, knowing that it will send her over the edge.

She screams out, her body giving a massive shudder, her heels digging into the small of my back.

I let her ride all the way down until she's a puddle on the bed and then I finally lift up, climbing off the bed long enough to shuck off the rest of my clothes.

I pause, standing next to the bed as I look down at Charlotte. Her eyes are half closed, her thighs still parted, her body languid as she reaches a hand toward me. The pink diamond catches the light and I grab her hand, pulling it toward my mouth.

She partially sits up so that her palm can reach my lips and I finger the ring as I kiss each fingertip.

That ring is supposed to be there.

I'm still touching the ring when she tips forward, sinking her mouth around the head of my cock.

A guttural growl rumbles up my throat as I drop my chin so that I can watch her take me in.

God, she's so beautiful. Her ass is still red, her legs half folded underneath her as she takes all of me in, her lips coming all the way to my base where my cock meets my body.

I hear her give a little choke, but she doesn't stop.

It's so incredibly hot that my vision blurs as I sink my fingers into the silky strands of her hair.

I don't push or pull her. This is Charlotte's to do however she wants. She holds for a second, two, until she finally slowly slides off only to dive back in.

Over and over she takes me all the way into her mouth, the slow pace of it making my balls tighten as I threaten to erupt.

I hold it off as long as I can because this is everything. I can't put into words why it's different, but I know it is.

Her name comes out broken and jagged as I lose the fight to hold off, my cum exploding from my cock as she swallows it all down, her wet eyes looking up into mine as she does.

Both my hands are now in her hair, our gazes locked together as she drains me dry.

She falls back on the bed, her hands landing over her head, and I follow, climbing up her until we're chest to chest, hip to hip, her legs wrapped about me, my arms covering hers, our fingers lacing together.

"No more going out until this business is all done," I say right before I kiss her swollen mouth.

"All right," she answers, her eyes fluttering closed.

My sweet sexy Charlotte. Even after the orgasm has rung me dry, I want more of her. I'm insatiable when it comes to this woman.

"I can't have you hurt, sweetheart," I whisper, knowing that if something happened to her, it would break me.

"I won't be," she sighs out, her head lilting to the side. "You'll keep me safe."

Fuck me.

Her neck is exposed for me to trail several kisses down its long, creamy column. Our fingers are knotted together, my cock already half at attention because it's needy like that.

Her body is so relaxed, I think she might actually be asleep, until she shifts under me. "How did Jackson know Professor Burke's name? I didn't tell him."

My muscles go rigid and in return, I feel her stiffen as she turns to me. "How did he know which building my classes were in?"

"Charlotte."

Her hand, the one with the pink diamond pulls from mine. "How did he know, Mason?"

I could lie. But I'm not that man. I've committed my fair share of sins, but I consider myself above fibbing to the woman who is wrapped around me. "I had you followed."

She gasps, pushing out from my embrace. I let her go, rolling onto my side as she rushes off the bed, standing to face me.

I know this is bad. And normally my triage brain would be working through all the scenarios. Figuring out the words that would minimize the damage.

But I'm too satiated, and honestly, just distracted by how gorgeous she looks when she's angry. Her high full tits are staring at me, the length of her flat stomach accentuated with small muscle lines. Her hips have the perfect flare and don't even get me started on the thighs that have spent a great deal of time wrapped around my head.

I know this is a problem. Charlotte is dulling all my senses and that has always been the danger of allowing a woman into my life like this.

"You had me followed?" she gasps, shaking her head. "Why would you do that?"

"Because," I reach my hand out to her but she doesn't take it. Hers are firmly planted on her hips. "At first, I thought you might tell people that I owned the club. I cleaned a crime scene, it was a problem, you knowing who I was."

"How do people not know that already?"

"Shell company."

She shakes her head, as if she's just realizing that she's mixed up with a bad man. I never claimed to be the good guy. "And after you realized that I wouldn't talk?"

That is trickier and I'm not sure how much I should admit. I don't want to her to walk away, don't want to scare her. "You're mine to protect Charlotte. You have been for a while."

Her mouth opens and then closes, indecision marking her features as her brows pucker together. But her hands slip from her hips, falling to her sides as she looks away.

I'm up then, standing in front of her. "Tell me what you're thinking."

"That this is messed up."

She's not wrong. Have the two of us ever made sense? Ever fit into something that might actually work?

I'm not sure.

But I take her hand, the one with my ring on her finger and I bring it to my lips. Because I'm obsessed and it's only getting worse.

Sinking my cock into her isn't going to cure me, I already know that I'm only going to want her more.

I'm still going to do it because I'm tired of denying myself, and now that I've had her here, I can't get off on reports that Jackson gives me. They used to be my little hit of dopamine. *She's taking this class. Turned another boy down*. But that won't be enough anymore.

I can't let her go even if it means I'm burning us both to the ground. "I'm not saying you're wrong," I whisper before I hook her waist and pull her close. "But also, there was a reason I've gone to great lengths to protect you, sweetheart."

"And what is that?"

Her chest pushes against mine, her soft belly pressing to my hips. My fingers are in her hair again, my lips on her temple. "I want you in my bed."

I feel the slight wince, the downturn of her mouth. Did my answer not satisfy? It's the most I can admit to her and to myself. But she slides out of my arms and into the bed.

It's enough.

I climb in behind her and pull her tight to my chest.

That's when I realize the water is still running in the shower. I am fucking up all the details. The question is, in this war where I am supposed to be king and Charlotte a pawn, I wonder how much I'm willing to sacrifice to protect her, keep her on the board.

Because I can feel how much ground I am losing. A few hours ago, I was swearing to myself I'd let her go when this business was done. And now, I'm laying here thinking of every way I can keep her.

She's asleep before I even say a word, so I just slip out of the bed, turn off the water, and climb back into the sheets, pulling her close again.

I've got to find a way to do this better. Keep Charlotte and keep my head. Both our lives depend on it.

CHAPTER NINETEEN

CHARLOTTE

I WAKE THE NEXT MORNING, Mason still asleep in the bed next to me. My heart gives a painful throb as I try to remember why my chest is hurting…

And then I remember.

Mason had me followed for actual years. It's the invasion of privacy, I think at first. Then again, if I could have had him followed, I probably would have.

But then the second deeper reason his actions upset me… I was barely surviving. He saw all of it and did…nothing.

What had changed? Why had he suddenly intervened?

I mean, besides me almost getting killed. Maybe that's what forced him to come to my defense. But I'd been living in a slum and I was being harassed by my professor and he'd remained out of sight.

I slide back the covers and creep from the bed, getting my camera. I don't know why, but I need it now to understand what is bothering me. Sitting back on my side, I point the lens, getting a picture of his knee and powerful thigh bent into a relaxed position as it sticks out of the sheet.

Then, his elbow above his head.

Peeling back the covers, I take a picture of his bare hip, the way it juts out, surrounded by muscle.

"What are you doing?"

I'm now kneeling over him, camera to my eye, completely naked. I drop the camera down a few inches, wincing in guilt. "Sorry."

He smiles at me, that sexy grin and I lift the camera, taking a picture of his mouth before I point the camera lower, capturing the space just below his belly button and then I go higher to his biceps.

I'm not methodical with art. The light catches my eye or a movement or a shape. I feel my pictures, I don't think about them.

When I'm done snapping, I hand Mason the camera. I know he wants to see. I climb off the bed, and head to the shower in my room.

"Where are you going?"

"To the shower," I call over my shoulder.

"I want you in my shower."

I look back at him, wrinkling my nose. I usually heed the command I hear in his voice. I'm not one for arguing but I'm still trying to figure out what's bothering me, besides the obvious, he spied on me. It's deeper but I can't quite articulate it yet. "I like my shampoo better."

Later, I'll look at the pictures and see what they make me feel.

I hear him get up and follow, but I cross into my room and into my smaller bathroom. I nearly snort, remembering how my entire apartment could fit into the smaller bathroom.

Mason is still behind me. He sets my camera on the vanity, I hear it on the surface, before he comes into the bathroom.

I turn on the water, wondering how I'm going to handle this. I haven't been this cautious with Mason since that first night and I don't know how to keep my feelings to myself.

He steps in behind me, picking up the shampoo bottle on the shelf.

"What are you doing?"

"Taking note of the brand," he says eyeing the bottle. "If this is the thing that keeps you out of my shower..."

"What?"

"I'll have to stock the other room."

That makes me smile. But it quickly slips off my face. "How long do you think I'll be here?"

He steps up behind me, nosing my hair as his arms snake around my waist. "I'm close to closing the permits for the tunnels. After that, the Italians are going to start striking out for revenge. I'm about to really piss them off, not that I care."

"But the Italians are the ones I saw getting murdered, right?" Why would they want to hurt me? I'm their witness.

"Right," he says sliding his hands up my skin. Despite the warm water, my skin pebbles with goosepimples at his touch. He always feels good.

And when he cups my breast in both hands, I gasp. He tweaks one of my nipples, his lips sucking at my neck. I could lose myself in his embrace.

"Does that mean they are not a danger to me?"

His hands still. "Considering they killed my father, I can assure you that they are a danger to everyone."

I spin in his arms, my gasp lost in the heavy steam of the air. "Oh, Mason. I didn't know..."

He pulls me close, his body wrapped around mine. "I know you didn't."

There is so much more I want to ask. What happened with his father? What are his plans for me? Now and later...

I wrap my arms about his neck. Knowing they killed his father has pushed my concerns to the back of my thoughts, my focus now on what's happened to him. "I don't understand your world. How can you do business with those men if they did that to you?"

"I don't do business with them. Not really. And this tunnel will allow me to finally repay them for all they've done."

I'm still not sure how I fit into that, but I lean back, searching his face. This is about revenge for him. And I'm part of that...I see it now.

My stomach sinks deeper. Does he just not want me to help the Italians? Or is there something more? It would make sense that he wouldn't want me to be a witness for his Italian rivals to use to strike out against the Dukes. Is that why he's suddenly protecting me?

He's kissing my neck even as he reaches back and gets the soap. "I'd like to stay in this shower all day, but I've got a long day pushing the building permits through."

Part of me aches to lose his touch but the other part is relieved.

In the last twenty-four hours, things have gotten so complicated. Then I shake my head. They were always complicated. The change is that I no longer see this as just an exchange.

My body, it belongs to Mason. Even now, it aches under his large hands as they soap up every inch of my body.

"A day with the zoning department," I wrinkle my nose. "The only thing more boring might be staying here alone all day."

He's bending down, washing each of my legs. "It won't be forever. Today is a big step forward."

"And then you'll get your revenge and I'll..." I leave it blank. Waiting to hear what he'll fill in.

His hands slow. "We'll figure that out after you're not in danger."

That does not make me feel any better. But he turns on the other shower head and begins soaping his own body. He's all business now, a model of cold efficiency, and I watch him having that feeling again that I'd jumped from the frying pan into the fire.

Mason might just burn me alive.

"Mason?"

He stops scrubbing his hair to turn to me. "Yes?"

"Can I have groceries delivered?" I need to keep my hands busy today. It'll help me to sort through my feelings.

"You don't have enough food?"

"No. I..." I grab the shampoo, squirting some into my hand and lifting my hand over my head to scrub my hair.

Without warning, he's back in front of me, his hand around my waist, his mouth sucking in one of my nipples.

I toss my head back, arching into his mouth as I gasp out. "I wanted to cook."

"That's fine," he says between sucks. "As long as you promise I get you for dessert."

"Promise," I gasp. At this rate, I'm never going to figure out a thing. He's a distraction that has my senses all addled.

Slowly, he pulls away again with a sigh. "I've got to go, princess. But I'm holding you to your promise."

"Princess?" My brows lift as I finish washing out the shampoo, applying conditioner. "That's a new one." Roman had called me that the first night. I wonder what it means…

"I guess it is," he says with one last kiss before he turns back to his shower. I finish too and then we both climb out, Mason wrapping me in a fluffy white towel.

We leave the bathroom as he starts for his bedroom. He stops, looking at my vanity, a brow quirking. "Do you see what I'm seeing?"

I scrunch my brow. "What?"

He walks over to the vanity, picking up my gloss. "You left this out of place."

I blink in surprise. I haven't been able to do that in years. Walking to the vanity, I take the lip gloss from his hand and slide it into the proper slot on the tray.

"What does that mean?" he asks.

I shake my head. Is it good or bad that I'm relaxing in his home? I don't know, so I use his favorite line, "We'll talk more tonight. Someone has to go to work."

He kisses me then, long and slow and full of promise. "Tonight."

I look down at the ring shining back up at me. Twisting it on my finger, I wonder what it all means. The fake engagement, the real feelings, the mysterious motivations. Mason is not an easy man, that's for sure.

My phone lights up as Mason sends me an app for groceries.

I nip at my lip even as I cross to my closet and dig out my crappy old phone. It's run out of charge, and I plug it in before I go into the bathroom to dry my hair.

When I come out, I quickly dress, skipping the makeup for now as I fire up my old phone.

Gus has called asking me when I'm coming in and Kim has left me like nine messages.

I told her that I wouldn't be in that first day, but I can see why she's worried. We usually talk every day.

Not even thinking I dial her number.

"Where the hell have you been?" She asks by way of greeting.

It actually makes me smile. She's worried. I've missed her. "It's such a long story. How are you?"

"Crappy." But I hear her smile. "Gus has me working doubles so I can barely get into the studio."

"Where are you now?"

"Getting ready to head into Rebel's. I can only assume that since you don't care about work, you're actually graduating."

"I am."

"Good for you," she gushes and I know she means it. We're planning to go to New York together, though she has a summer course to take. Time at the dance studio has put her behind schedule. "One more piece of our plan is in place."

"Working extra will help you too," I offer weakly. As much as she needs money, she also needs rehearsal time if she's going to get into a reputable dance company.

"You know I love you, but since you left, Gus has us working doubles every day to cover for you and he is not happy about it, either."

My smile grows. This conversation is just so…normal. "Gus is going to be so disappointed when I quit."

"Charlotte, I know how quiet you can be, but I don't have time to draw it out of you. Spill now."

With a deep breath, I try to think about what I'm going to say. I can't tell her everything. It's too dangerous. "I started seeing a guy."

"You're ditching your life for a guy? You? Are you changing your mind about New York?"

I shake my head. She's not wrong. "It's a long story, and I can't tell you all of it now, but I am not changing my mind about New York, though it might be a moot point because, while I really like him, I'm not sure if he feels the same about me."

Kim sucks her teeth, the sound filling the phone line. "I wish I could come see you."

I can't tell her that's not even possible. "Me too."

"But you can start by pressing him for information. I know you and you haven't." She is totally right. "If he's shady in his answers, he's not legit."

"He's too alpha to be a liar, but he is a high roller and used to getting his way." Mason won't lie, but he might really avoid a question to suit his purposes. Sort of like the shower this morning where he didn't answer direct questions.

"That's great advice. Thanks, Kim."

"And I'm glad to hear your graduating. That was kind of touch and go with Professor Burke."

"Me too. Now we need to get you situated."

Kim lets out a long breath. It hasn't been easy for her either. "Listen, I have to go, but first, I just need to know. Are you okay?"

I nod, realize she can't see me, and then say. "Yeah. I'm good. I'm working on a few more of those bucket list items."

Kim laughs. "We've got our whole lives for a bucket list."

"True." I swallow down a lump. Some days, I wonder if that's true for me.

"Call me tomorrow?" she says in a rush, clearly racing out the door.

"I will. Love you."

"Love you too," she says, keys jingling, before she hangs up.

I sit at the vanity, staring at the gloss. I'd been feeling more relaxed yesterday then I had in years. I felt safe with Mason these past few days and I'd let down my guard.

I'd always known that Mason was a predator. What I'd always wondered, the question I couldn't allow myself to forget…was I his prey?

CHAPTER TWENTY

MASON

THE ENTIRE DAY, I'm trying to escape the pit of my stomach reaction that something is wrong.

I shouldn't feel this way.

My permits are pushed through in record time, everyone who needs to sign being present and accounted for, all inspections happening without a hitch.

By the end of the day, I'm the proud owner of digging rights in the Las Vegas sand.

This is a day I've spent two years preparing for and I should be ecstatic. But that pit of dread won't go away.

Roman is sitting next to me in the back seat of the car and he's been unusually quiet as well, especially considering the major victory we just had.

But I can't focus on him, or the fact that my family thinks I'm losing my mind, because my thoughts are consumed by Charlotte.

She was different this morning and I don't like it.

The guards she'd been letting down were back up and stronger than ever. Worse still, she was asking questions.

About my motivations. About the future.

None of them had nice answers. I scrub a hand through my hair, rubbing at my face. Roman looks over at me with a frown. "Are you going to tell me why you're in a shit mood after the day you just had?"

We might be brothers, but we don't exactly talk about feelings. "Probably not."

"Did you take my advice?"

I don't need to ask what he's referring to. "I don't want to talk about Charlotte."

"I do," he turns toward me then.

"Too bad."

He goes on like I haven't spoken at all. "Either you did not take my advice, in which case you are sexually frustrated, or the two of you got into some kind of fight."

"Neither," I say through gritted teeth.

His brows raise then. "Do tell."

"No."

Jackson's eyes meet mine in the rearview mirror. I don't take the limo on days like this because it's too ostentatious. When the inspectors see a vehicle like that, they will apply themselves to taking you down a peg or two and find a reason to create more red tape. They've got their own egos and who can blame them for wanting to take arrogant pricks down a peg? But right about now, I'd give anything for a privacy screen.

"Are you upset about that thing with the professor yesterday?" Jackson asks. "I can hire someone to have him killed. I've still got those old school connections from our mob days."

"The professor?" Roman asks, leaning forward, looking at Jackson and not me. He knows where he'll get answers. "What happened with the professor?"

"He got really handsy with Charlotte." Jackson answers for me. I swear, I'm going to punch them both when this car stops.

"And how did that make you feel?" Roman asks like he's my fucking therapist.

"Like I'm going to beat the shit out of you if you don't stop talking."

Both Jackson and Roman laugh.

"I can fire you," I snarl at Jackson.

"But you won't," he answers unconcerned. And then he shifts his rearview mirror gaze to Roman. "He can't stop touching her. Got to have his hands on her all the time."

My skin crawls to hear Jackson speak like that. I am a man of infinite control. "Would you two stop acting like a couple of old women?" But I know the truth. They've both figured out that I am not in control at all when it comes to Charlotte. That I'm about to lose everything. I feel the truth crawling up my spine and I wait for Roman's inevitable questions. Who will take over when I come undone…

Only…neither seems that concerned.

"She is a looker," Roman nods, agreeing with his own words.

"Beautiful women are everywhere," I respond but I know it isn't true. No woman has ever affected me like Charlotte.

And Roman knows it too. "Soft, sweet, submissive," he adds, ticking off the list on his fingers.

"You know the rules just as well as I do."

"Mason, you're a fucking king. Make the rules, don't follow them."

I stare at him without a response because he's right. I made the rules to begin with…

Is it because Roman was younger when our father died that he isn't worried about my relationship with Charlotte? Because this is not at all what I expected.

My phone dings, Charlotte's name popping up. She's asking about purchasing a photo album. I stare at the message, shaking my head.

I've been worried about the woman all day and now I'm getting this totally benign message about photo albums?

I send a message back telling her to forward me a link from

Amazon. The three dots appear and I wait, realizing I'm holding my breath. What the hell is wrong with me?

I WANT *to buy it myself. Can I have it shipped here? Do you not want my name on packages? I could give you money.*

I STARE AT THE SCREEN. She doesn't even have a job and I'm worth well over a billion dollars? This is a ridiculous conversation, and also, why would she not want me to buy it for her?

I'm back to worried. Who's the old woman now?

My fingers fly over the screen as I start to fire back a text that says as much when Roman begins laughing. I look over at him, my stare so fierce, he stops laughing, but he's still grinning. "What?" I bark.

"Just admit you've fallen hard."

I snort but that knot in my stomach only tightens, expanding to my chest. Because Roman is right. "We don't do love."

Roman shrugs, settling back into his seat as Jackson pulls into the garage in my building. He'll drop me and then take Roman home. It's how we usually do these sorts of things and I know that both Roman and Jackson have noted how eager I am to return to my apartment.

I just fucking missed Charlotte, and what's more, we have several things to talk about. It might be time to come clean and to maybe move forward? I have no idea what that even looks like.

On the one hand, I've spent almost my entire adult life building this business and I know it means losing the support of Jake, Luke, and fucking Leo if I choose Charlotte.

On the other…my life would feel hollow and empty without her. I'm starting to be able to admit that to myself.

Which is crazy. I haven't even been inside her yet. And yet, the signs have been there for a while. It's in the way I want her to wear my ring.

The way I can't keep my hands off her. The way I almost lost all my shit when that fucking Professor Burke tried to hurt her.

I get out of the car with hardly a goodbye and punch a button on my phone to open the elevator, typing in the new code.

The doors slide open and I step inside, letting out a long breath of air, trying to loosen my muscles.

The ride is short, and when I step out, an amazing smell hits my nose. It's Asian, but it's not salty soy sauce heavy, it's delicate and savory all in one.

Striding out of the hall, I find Charlotte in the kitchen, pale blue dress and a white apron adorning her body, her hair pinned back in a neat twist. Her feet are bare as she stands at the counter and the picture is just too much. It steals my breath.

"Hello," she smiles over her shoulder as she chops red peppers. "You're home early."

Home. It is my home. And with startling clarity I know for a fact that wherever my home is, Charlotte belongs there too.

I step up behind her, holding her hips in my hands as I place a soft kiss where her neck meets her shoulder.

She stiffens and I know whatever was between us this morning, is still there. It's time to clear that shit.

I want Charlotte to be warm and comfortable in my arms. I want her to be safe, and I'll do whatever it takes to give that to her.

I don't take my hands away, if anything I tighten them, giving her a squeeze before I slide my arms around her waist. "Whatever your making smells unbelievable."

She relaxes a bit. "That's good."

"Where did you learn to cook like this?" I'm well aware of what her budget has been.

She shrugs, picking up the knife and starting her preparations again. "Not many Asian restaurants in Nebraska. And you know me, I like things just so."

It's true. She has the eyes for detail that can elevate anyone in life. I sweep my hands down her belly and then back around her hips, kissing a trail along her neck. I breathe in her scent.

Here's the truth.

I built this business from the ground up. My dad was in debt. I scraped the money together to buy that first club, made it a massive success so that I could get the collateral to buy another and another.

And the shell company. It was originally to hide us from the Italians and Toni Carcetti.

In those early days, it was my sheer force of will that made us a success. If my family wants to take my empire away from me, I'll let them have it. Then, I'll build another. And this time, I've got several assets that are in my name alone. Like this building. In and of itself, it's worth a small fortune. I won't be starting from negative, and I won't need anyone's help.

If I'm headed down the same path as my father, to death and destruction, then I'm going to die happy.

I think of Charlotte that first night. When she'd kneeled before me and told me she was ready to die, just as long as it was me who did it.

I suck in my breath, straightening up. She was ready to end it with me right then. I think I might finally be there too. If I'm headed to my end, she's going to be next to me.

"What's wrong?" she asks, her brow scrunched as she looks over her shoulder again.

I give her a smile. No malice, nothing but joy. "Not at thing, princess. Not a damned thing. In fact…"

My phone rings, shrill and loud from my pocket, and I lift it out to send the call to voicemail. I don't care who it is…

But Roman's name has my brow scrunching as I debate whether or not to answer.

We were just together. He wouldn't be calling unless there was a problem.

Keeping my other hand on Charlotte's hip, I keep her ass firmly in the cradle of my hips as I pick up. "What?"

But Roman doesn't snark back. Instead, he lets out a loud breath of air. "It's Leo and it's bad…"

CHAPTER TWENTY-ONE

MASON

MY HEART STUTTERS in my chest. As angry as I still am at Leo, he is my brother. "What's happened?"

Charlotte's knife clatters to the counter and she's spinning to face me. She must have heard the worry in my voice because it's now written all over her face. I hook her waist pulling her close, which is her cue to wrap her arms around my chest.

"Fuck. I don't even know where to begin," Roman says and his voice actually shakes.

My throat closes along with my eyes. "Tell me."

"He went on a bender last night. Hopping from casino to casino, hitting all the major families and making a ruckus. Spent millions. Broke things. Pissed everyone off. And now..."

If I have to identify my brother's body...

"Roman." My voice is so rough that it comes out as a growl. I know this shit is hard to say but I need to hear it and then I can start making a plan. Figure out how to bail Leo out of whatever shitstorm in which he's landed.

"He's missing."

I start like I've been hit, and Charlotte tightens her hold around me. I squeeze her tighter too, dropping my face into her shoulder and squeeze my eyes shut. Leo can't be dead. There's too much to fucking say.

I need to tell him what an asshole he is but also…that he's my asshole brother and I actually love him no matter what he does.

Charlotte doesn't say anything, but I realize she's holding up my weight, her body pressed between me and the counter.

She's spread her hands out on my back, her chin on my shoulder as she presses a light kiss to my neck.

Every part of her body is comforting me and in that moment some truths are crystal clear. I've been wondering how this might end. How I give her up when I want her more and more and the answer is as obvious as a high rise on the strip. I don't give her up. Ever. Charlotte is the woman meant to be at my side forever.

"Mason?" Roman asks, and I realize I've been silent, not saying a word.

"Bring everyone here. Fifteen minutes."

Roman pauses. "Your apartment? You're sure you don't want to go to the conference room at Kincaid?"

"Here." And then I hang up. I've got my reasons, not that I'm articulating them exactly. But I'm not leaving Charlotte alone, and she's starting to feel like my family. Which means, she's meeting the family today. Whatever they decide about Leo, about me, Charlotte is part of this.

I'm kissing Charlotte before I've even thought it through, my mouth devouring hers like I'm trying to draw some strength from her.

She's pliant in my arms, giving me everything I need and want, her body molding to me. "Mason," she whispers between kisses. "I…"

"Don't say anything. Just kiss me." I hold her jaw in my hand, looking down into those grey eyes. "I just need you to kiss me, Charlotte."

She pushes up on her tiptoes, her lips pressing to mine, long and sweet, the pressure of her soft mouth helping to close the tear in my chest. My hand slides to the back of her neck as I taste her over and over like a man dying of thirst. Because I am... At least I'm dying for her.

I pull back and that's when I see tears shimmering on her lashes. One falls, tracking down her cheek. With my thumb, I brush it away. "Don't cry."

She shakes her head. "I'll never forgive myself if Leo—"

I cover her mouth with my thumb. "Listen to me. If Leo chose to go shooting off last night, that is not your fault. We've all got our father's demons living inside of us and that is not anything you can control."

Her lips part as though she might argue. "I never wanted to hurt Leo."

"Leo's problem has never been about you, sweetheart. You went out a few times years ago. This has always been about me."

She looks up at me with wet lashes as another tear slips down her cheek. "That night at the club, I was working my way up to telling him that I didn't think we should go out again. I'm no good at confrontation but if I'd just said it...."

Has she been beating herself up over hurting Leo? "I know you don't like confrontation. Your professor aside, you leave a situation before you fight."

Her eyes widen, but I lean down and kiss her lips. I'm not trying to hurt her with her own truths today. I just want her to understand. "Leo was going to sleep with you and then end it the next day. It's his modus operandi, right down to bringing you to family dinner. He does it all the time."

She blinks up at me as I continue, needing her to understand. "Like I said, he's never been upset about you and none of this is your fault. He's pissed that I haven't given him more power at Kincaid Enterprises. You were one small cut in a large gaping wound."

Her shoulders slump. "That's good because I would hate myself for getting in between you and your brother. As someone who went without one, I know how important family is in this world. I'd never hurt yours."

I squeeze her again, kissing her temple. Her words are sweet, and I appreciate them, but even more than that, I realize Charlotte does need a family and that is going to be me.

My phone chimes and I look down to see that Roman has already arrived downstairs.

I push the button to open the elevator, but I don't let Charlotte go. "How much dinner did you make?"

"Too much," she answers, a small smile pulling at her mouth. "I can't seem to cook small."

I touch the corner of her mouth with my thumb. I can't get enough of her, even these small touches. "Good. I'm glad you made too much because these guys are always hungry."

She nods and then slowly turns back to the counter and picks up the knife to keep chopping.

I don't back up though, and when the elevator opens, I've still got my hands on her hips, my front pressed to her back.

I'm making a statement and it's one I know all the guys understand as they stop in the kitchen. Even if Leo is pissed about Charlotte, she belongs here with me, in my arms, and that isn't changing. I love my brother and I'll help him however I can, but Charlotte isn't going anywhere.

"Isn't this the picture of domesticity," Jake says, his normally dry sarcasm on full display as he steps to the front of group. "I'm Jake. Nice to meet you, Charlotte."

Charlotte pauses her chopping, tilting her chin up to smile at Jake. "And you." She sets down the knife and extends her hand to my uncle's.

I tighten my grip, knowing that I'm showing my possessive side. I don't like the way Jake is taking in every fucking detail. Why did I have to get Charlotte dresses that fit her so perfectly? I can see Jake taking in her glossy hair, amazing rack, flat belly, long legs, right down to her bare feet. Even her toes are adorable.

"I'm Luke," my cousin calls from just behind Jake. "What smells so good?"

"Charlotte's cooking," I say, like that isn't obvious, my hands tracing her hips in a clear act I want everyone to notice. "We'll leave her to it and head into my study."

Luke is craning his neck, not to check out Charlotte, but what she's got cooking on the stove. He sniffs at the boiling pot and then glances at the saucepan. "Will there be leftovers?"

"There's plenty," Charlotte says with another smile. It's good that she's charming them. It might help. I still hate it, but I recognize the importance.

"How can you think about food?" I rumble as we make our way into my study. It's a man's room with leather and dark wood and built in bookshelves. There are a few pictures in the tray from the new high-end printer I bought for Charlotte and I make a note to check them out later.

"I'd like to start by saying that I'm sure Leo is fine," Jake says. "I know no one has talked to him but that fucker is indestructible. He's just sleeping it off in some hotel penthouse suite while we're all getting our knickers in a twist."

I nod, hoping he's right. "Let's assume that's true. How big of a mess did he make while on his bender?"

"Let's see. He went to the sole casino the Dukes have and tossed a hundred large onto the casino floor starting a complete frenzy in the crowd that took both hotel security and several cops to sort out. Then he made his way to the favorite gambling floor of the Russians and tipped a slot machine, breaking it wide open. And finally, he went to the biggest casino the Italians own and started a brawl in his own special way. Ten were taken to the hospital. Tons of bad press for them. Again, cops and guards alike had to end the fight... You get the picture."

"Fuck me." I run a hand through my hair. "That's a big mess."

"He's trying to get someone's attention, that's for sure." Roman gives me a long look and then begins pacing, his hands combing through his hair before he scrubs at his face.

"He pissed off every major family in Las Vegas and now he's missing in action," Luke adds. "I've called him like five times but he's not picking up."

I pull out my phone and try to do the same, but I go straight to his voicemail. "We have people out looking for him?"

"We do. But worse…" This is Jake who answers. "The other families want a meeting to discuss reparations for his actions."

"Fuck. We haven't had one of those since dad's death." Inwardly, I clench. The last meeting was the one where I got told if I wanted to save my family, I'd stay quiet and I'd stay in my lane. There would be no retribution for me.

Not that I want to be a gangster. That has never been my way. Even now, I plan to make the Italians pay through completely legal means.

But they are still going to pay. And I don't need them being pissed before they even know I'm cutting them out of the chain of casinos.

"What was Leo thinking?" I'm gripping my phone so tightly, I can't believe I haven't broken it.

"He wasn't. That's always been his problem."

I shake my head. "I'm not so sure. He's cock-blocked my tunnel. If the Italians are already pissed and they find out that I'm shutting down their business, they might go nuclear. He's made a move against me."

Luke says as he shakes his head. "You think so? It's not like him to plan. I think it's more likely Leo is working his way up to a finish worthy of your father."

But I grimace with that one. "We're all suffering from that, aren't we?"

"You?" Jake asks, pulling out a cigar from his pocket.

"Don't even think about lighting that thing in my house." I point my finger. "And I know you're all thinking that the way I'm acting with Charlotte is just like my father." I've been thinking the same thing.

But they all blink back at me, not an accusation between them.

"What you're doing with Charlotte is nothing like Dad," Roman says with a shake of his head as though it's completely obvious.

"Your dad fucked another boss's wife and he wasn't even quiet about it all while he racked up giant debts all over town trying to impress her." Jake knew more about his brother's death then even I did. And he might be even more pissed about it than me. He's got his own plans for revenge, and I don't get involved with them. That's his business.

Luke is nodding. "Granted, your relationship with Charlotte isn't completely complication-free, but they never are." Luke shrugs. "Leo aside, you've picked an available woman who seems to suit you."

Roman steps up to him, clapping him on the shoulder. And then his gaze meets mine. "We were fools to make that pact and, if we're all being honest, we did it for Leo's benefit. He was always the one who was liable to follow in dad's footsteps."

"Speak for your fucking self." Jake curls his lip. "I'm single for life, pact or no."

I'm not talking because I'm speechless. We've never spoken like this and I'm honestly shocked that they don't seem bothered by my relationship with Charlotte. I'd just assumed...

"The point is..." Roman stresses. "Every kingdom needs a queen. And honestly, I'm starting to wonder if a little softness, that a woman might provide, might not ease some of the tension and actually keep us from making mistakes like Leo did last night. If Dad had still been married to Mom..."

My phone dings again. I look down, Charlotte's name appearing on my screen.

Dinner is ready whenever you're ready to eat.

"Who's hungry?" I ask, trying to dial Leo again. Nothing. Straight to voicemail.

Jake, Luke, and Roman leave the study before me as I try to call my brother one more time. I follow behind watching as they each grab a bowl of noodles from the counter and take a seat at the table.

They dig in without a word, but I make my way around the island running my hand over Charlotte's arm.

Her eyes hold a question even as she allows me to pull her against my body. I wrap my arms around her, my lips kissing that spot just below her ear, my nose in her hair. "You look beautiful," I whisper.

Her hands come to my biceps, pink staining her cheeks. "Mason, they're watching," she whispers.

"Let them." I don't give a shit. Charlotte is mine and my family already knows it.

But I don't have a chance to tell her.

Because a deafening blast shakes the building to its core.

CHAPTER TWENTY-TWO

Mason

I've got Charlotte on the ground under the protection of my body in a second, one arm under her back the other cradling her head as drywall from the ceiling rains down a fine dust on top of us.

This building is built to withstand a nuclear bomb, perk of being a real estate mogul, but I have to wonder what the fuck that was? Earthquake? Attack?

"Hellfire," Jake snarls from the table. "What just happened?"

No one answers. No one knows.

"You and Charlotte all right?" Luke asks, his voice sounding muffled.

"Fine. You?"

"We're all good," he says.

"Does the elevator work?" Roman asks. Is he talking to me?

I don't get up, keeping Charlotte under me as I lift my head to look around. I can't see any of them around the island. "Check."

Roman passes by me, half crouched as he pushes the button, the doors slide open. He looks back at me, shaking his head in disbelief.

"And I thought you were crazy when you spent so much building this place that no one lives in but you."

I don't smile back. "Luke," I bark, rolling to the side and taking Charlotte with me. "Go down with him. Find out what's happened."

Luke appears without a word, joining Roman in the elevator. I knew I wouldn't get pushback because we're all soldiers. The doors close and the two of them disappear. I don't mean to put them in danger but I'm not leaving Charlotte's side if we're under attack.

Jake comes to squat next to us. "Charlotte all right?"

"I'm fine," she answers, her hands flexing on my back.

Slowly, I start to get up, pulling her with me. She's covered in the same dust as everyone else, but she looks all right other than that. Sitting on the floor, I pull her into my lap and start checking her body for injuries. I run my hands over her legs, down her arms, circling her ribs, watching her face for winces of pain.

She's fine, not showing any signs of injury...but I can't make my hands stop. I run them over every inch of her again, even weaving them into her hair to check her skull.

"Mason," she says quietly. "I'm all right."

In answer, I pull her close, kissing her head.

"Not a crier, eh?" Jake asks.

She shakes her head as she answers. "I cry as much as the next girl, I guess. But to be honest, this pales in comparison to when Roman found me in that alley. Or when my dad died."

Jake cracks a small smile. "Warrior wounds and a fighting heart. Got it." And then his gaze meets mine and he gives me the tiniest jerk of his chin to show his approval.

Maybe the kingdom really does need a queen. And maybe my men are in agreement about who she should be.

In the distance I hear sirens, and I know I'm going to need to speak with the police. Roman and Luke appear once again, the elevator sliding open. "By the looks of it, pipe bomb in the parking garage."

"Bomb?" I say, standing up with Charlotte in my arms. "Are you kidding me?"

Roman scratches at his jaw. "With the nest that Leo stirred yesterday, it could be anyone."

"Tipping over a slot machine hardly seems worthy of bombing my building."

"Unless a certain family also found out that you were holding a witness for one of their family's murder victims. Or that you got permits for your tunnel."

It could be the permits, but then again, my brother might have let information about Charlotte slip…

But my blood is pumping at the idea, the tingle that I'm right pulsing through me. Yeah, my instincts are kicking in, the ones that never fail me and all of them are telling me that Leo is involved with what just happened.

If he endangered Charlotte's life, my fists clench against Charlotte's back, *the lives of every member of this family, I'll have his head.*

I rise, holding her in my arms still. "As soon as the police leave, you find Leo. I'm going to start making calls…" It was time I personally spoke to the other families. Time they understood.

If tested, I would wipe them all out. I kept myself within the bounds of the law because I could. Because I chose to do so.

Did Leo want to unleash the crazy? I have a deep well and now I have an even bigger reason to fight. I drop a kiss on Charlotte's head, my hold not easing up. Let anyone of them try and test me. They'd learn just how much grit held me together.

"You're not going to help us find Leo?" Jake's gaze slides to the way I'm holding Charlotte. He knows…knows that I've made a choice. Maybe I am embracing my old man's brand of crazy after all.

But I can't fight it anymore, and what's more, only my Kincaid insanity is going to top Leo's.

"No. But when you find him, if you find him, I want to see him." My hand spreads out on Charlotte's hip. "Immediately. Am I clear?"

"Clear," Jake nods.

Her hand is resting on my chest. "Do you need to look for Leo too?"

I can see the worry in her eyes, and I give her a small kiss on the tip of her nose. "I'm staying here with you."

"I'll be all right, Mason. He's your brother. You should—"

"I'm staying here," I repeat by way of answer. This is not up for debate. There is no way I'm leaving her.

The phone dings and I pull it out to see the police have arrived.

"If anyone asks, Charlotte is Charlotte Kincaid. Even if the Italians know she's here, we're not making her last name public and every man who learns her identity will know that she is mine. Messing with her means messing with me."

Charlotte starts against me, and Jake's eyebrows rise, but I don't care. My priorities have never been clearer.

The next two hours are a long parade of police officers and firefighters, the building being declared safe.

The floors under me are apartments that are still shells or are built out but are empty. At some point, I'll sell them off but, as the only current resident, the building is easy to check for damage.

When Luke, Jake, and Roman leave, I kiss Charlotte and head to my study, beginning the process of reaching out to the other families. No one knows anything, of course. And everyone is so pleasant on the phone.

Except for one man…

Toni Carcetti sounds as smug as a man possibly can. Yeah, I know the fucker lit the bomb. And I'll add this one to his list of debts.

The Dukes swear to help in any way they can. The Russians are cordial but cold.

I expected that. I, however, make it known to each of them that information will be highly rewarded by means of debt forgiveness or increased real estate, and that silence will mean debts are called in, traffic to their establishments cut off.

Everyone in this town owes me money. Everyone. I made sure of that a long time ago and I'll use it to my advantage now.

I don't mention the tunnel. I don't have to. They all know by now and I don't need to be specific. That will come later when I really start applying the pressure.

As I talk, I hear Charlotte about the apartment. She's humming as she works, restoring order to the chaos. The vacuum runs for close to an hour before things finally go silent.

But listening to her actually sharpens my focus. I think back to her tiny apartment, the one made beautiful, and I know she's out there reordering our home as I make certain we are safe.

It's a different version of Charlotte tending a home, and yet somehow exactly what I pictured in that moment when I'd stepped into her little place. The rest of Vegas, my brother Leo, they have not begun to see how hard I'll fight to preserve her world, our world.

Leaving my study, I head toward her room, the apartment already spotless. I stop and take it in, every surface is clean, and the dinner I never ate is packed away. I pull out the container taking several bites, the food excellent even cold and covered in a bit of drywall.

Stuffing the rest back in the fridge, I make my way into her room just as the shower turns on. Who needs more food. I've got Charlotte for dinner. "Princess?" I call before I open the door.

"Mason? In here," she calls back. I walk in just in time to see her tipping her head back into the spray, her arms over her head, her tits on full display.

For a moment I just drink her in. She's gorgeous like this and I just watch as she begins washing her hair. She catches my gaze and gives me a soft smile.

I need to move her into the other bedroom with me. Get the rest of her stuff from her place. But that is a problem for a quieter time.

I shrug my shirt off, not waiting for an invitation. This is my woman and I have every intention of fully and completely claiming her.

CHAPTER TWENTY-THREE

CHARLOTTE

SOMETHING WAS different with Mason tonight, but I wasn't sure what had changed. He always touched me, but today…

His hands have been all over me since he's been home. And when he'd worried I'd been hurt as he'd touched me everywhere multiple times.

Even in front of his family, I'd been crushed against him the entire time. I don't know much about dating, but I suspect that men who didn't care do not take such pains to be close, especially if something else might have drawn away their attention.

Something like a bombing.

The absurdity of that washed over me even as I tipped my head back in the water. Was I the target? Or had my association with Mason brought even more trouble my way? Was that even possible?

Without him, I'd likely be dead.

I shiver in the warm water and that's when the shower door opens.

Mason steps in, the rippling muscles of his body making my breath catch. "Hi."

"'Lo," he murmurs as he closes the door and then closes the distance between us. He's got me crushed against him, his mouth covering mine before I've barely taken a breath.

I cling to him as he kisses me over and over, his strength under my hands calming my racing heart.

"Are you all right, sweetheart?"

"I'm fine..." I know my breath catches on the words. I was fine. I held it together. Cleaned up the mess. "Or at least I was until I stepped into the shower."

He nods like that makes sense. "You were good as long as you were busy."

That's probably it. I slide my hands over the ridges of his biceps, the water making our skin slide in the most erotic way.

My worries start to fall away again, and when his mouth captures mine in a long kiss, I forget to be afraid.

Keep busy. Makes sense. Does Mason understand as he slides a hand from my waist down to my rear end, cupping it in his palm and pulling our hips tightly together? I can feel the strong press of his erection against my stomach as I use one of my legs to twist about his, binding us even tighter together.

My hands are in his hair, holding him as close as I can. I don't even realize I'm crying until he swipes a thumb over my cheek. "Charlotte."

"I'm all right. It's just water."

But his hands on my body ease, relaxing. "You have every right to cry, but I need you to know, I'm not letting anyone hurt you. Not now, not later, not ever."

The words make my chest tight. If I close my eyes, and I do, I could almost believe that what's been happening between us is real. Mason was so protective today because he cares.

I want to believe it so much because I know my feelings have definitely taken a turn. I'm pretty sure I'm falling in love.

My heart stutters at the realization and I pull back to look up at him, water from the rain head running down my face.

He reaches for my face, using his large palms to swipe the water away.

"Please don't let the Italians or the Dukes..." My voice catches again. I feel nearly as raw as I did that first night.

He's back to holding me tight. "You are mine, Charlotte. Mine to protect."

I nod. I know that. We have an agreement. "They were so close today."

Grabbing up the soap, he quickly washes me and then himself, shampooing the dust from his hair. My hands skim his body the entire time because touching him keeps me grounded, sane.

When he turns off the water, he opens the door, a rush of cool air filling the shower before he wraps me in a towel.

Then he lifts me in his arms, carrying me out of my room and into his. "Where are we going?"

"My bed," he answers. "It's larger and I think I'm moving you into my room anyway. We end up sleeping together every night regardless of where we both start."

I blink down at him, trying not to read too much into those words. But they sound like he's planning on me being here for a while. Hope replaces the fear.

"Why did you agree to have me pretend to be your fiancé? What do you get out of that arrangement?" I don't even think about it before I ask.

He stops in the middle of the room. "Your virginity. You know that."

His words are so plain that something in me unwinds, relaxes. "And after?"

"I told you in the shower. I'm not allowing anyone to hurt you ever, Charlotte."

More plain words that have me melting into him. My arms around his neck, my hands in his hair, I kiss him again, our tongues tangling together as the kiss grows and builds.

I barely feel when he lays me down on the bed but my thighs naturally part to accommodate him and as his hips settle between the softness of my thighs, I feel the hard length of him press against my seam.

We've never been closer to closing the deal, but I have another question and I tear my mouth from his. "Mason?"

"Yes, princess?"

"If you take my virginity tonight, I can stay with you after? At least until—"

"You can stay Charlotte," he answers, his gaze drilling into mine. His hand goes to the back of my knee, lifting my leg higher and opening my hips even more to him. "I told you, I'm not letting anyone hurt you. And here is the safest place for you tomorrow, and the next day, and the day after that."

I nod, feeling far better at his words as his hand slides up the back of my leg, his fingers only stopping when the tips are grazing my sex.

I forget to be afraid as lightning courses through me at his touch. Mason has always had this effect.

I'm a slave to the way he makes me feel and I forget all the reasons I should be worried when he starts touching me like this. But his fingers are only a light brush against my overheated flesh before they're gone again.

I give a small cry of frustration, wanting more of him. But he doesn't touch me again, instead, he chuckles next to my ear.

"Remember what I said. We only get to have your first time once. We're going to take it nice and slow because we are going to savor this, princess."

I circle his broad shoulders with my arms, sighing into his ear. "I know, I know. Patience. But I have been waiting forever. Like really, my entire adult life. It took me so long to find you and even after we met..."

He laughs then. "It has been a bumpy beginning, hasn't it?" He traces my collarbone with the tip of his index finger. "And I know you've been waiting. But we want this to be worth the wait."

Slowly, gently, he slides his hand up my body, over the towel, pulling out the tucked end and opening the fluffy fabric.

My breath catches as the cool air hits my torso, my nipples pebbling at the change in temperature.

His eyes fix on them and then be bends lower, sucking one into his mouth. I arch into the touch, gasping out my approval.

But not to favor one over the other, he moves to the other side, kissing and sucking his way to the already-erect tip of my other nipple.

It feels so good that I'm grinding against him, my legs locking about his hips, though the towel, still around his waist, keeps me from the contact I really crave.

He slides a hand down my rib cage and over my hip, settling his fingers between my legs. His touch is only a light brush still, through the curls and over the lips, but I shiver in pleasure wanting more.

How does he do this to me? My hands twist up in the sheets as he brushes down my length again, applying no more pressure and making me crazy as I thrust my hips up into his hand.

He finally increases the pressure even as he starts kissing a trail down my belly. One of my hands wraps around his neck, my fingers digging into his skin. I can still see the scratches I left last time, I try to ease the tension in my hand, so as not to draw blood again, but he feels so good.

"Go ahead and mark me," he rumbles as though he heard my thoughts. I don't ask how he knew, I just dig my fingernails into his skin, spreading my thighs wider to accommodate his shoulders.

His fingers are still sliding up and down my seam as he kisses the sensitive junction between stomach and leg and then moves lower to the inside of my thigh. Part of me wants him to give me the pleasure I am dying for inside, while another revels in these gentle touches and light kisses.

He's treating me like something precious. He has been all day today, and it's starting to mess with my head. How am I going to keep things straight? This is an arrangement born of necessity. He's not in love the way I am…

I'm dripping wet and squirming against him when he finally swipes his tongue against my clit. With a low moan, my nails dig into his neck, a keening cry ripping from my lips.

I'm so ready that it feels like I could orgasm at any second, but

Mason has settled into this light and easy rhythm that keeps me right on the edge.

I give a frustrated whimper, digging deeper into his neck. That's when he chuckles against me. "Who knew that my demure Charlotte would be so impatient?"

But I don't have to answer as he increases the pressure, sliding his fingers inside me so that my body tightens in the exact way I've been craving.

I'm mindless now, grinding against him as the first wave of the orgasm knocks into me, my breath exiting my lungs in a rush of air.

Wave after wave crashes into me until I'm so spent that I wilt into the bed. This was the mindlessness I've been craving all night.

But Mason isn't done. He climbs up my body using one hand to rip the towel off his waist and toss it on the floor in a single motion.

I would normally be impressed by the small display of athleticism but I'm too busy watching the predatory way he's climbing above me, and then there is the hard press of the head of his cock against my soft folds.

This is the moment I've been waiting for, but nerves make me tense again.

He slows, his elbows resting at my sides, his forearms running along my ribcage as his hands cradle my head. He kisses me long and slow, the taste of me on his lips and tongue.

I relax into that kiss. This is Mason and whatever else worries me, I've always trusted him with my body.

And that's the moment that he sinks inside me...

CHAPTER TWENTY-FOUR

MASON

CHARLOTTE FEELS LIKE HEAVEN...

She's soft and wet and so fucking tight, she grips my cock like nothing I've ever felt before.

She stiffens, clearly in pain, and I still, allowing her time to adjust.

I've been telling her that this should be special. I meant the words. But special doesn't even begin to describe what I feel in this moment. It's pleasure, so much goodness. But the slow movement is a bit of torture too.

I lean in to kiss her again, trying to help her relax, which will in turn ease the pain. I wait until I feel her soften and then slowly, I sink into her again until I'm finally fully inside her, my cock buried in her folds.

Christ, it feels so good. It takes everything in me to hold still, to allow her to adjust as I gently ease back out and then slowly push back in.

She's making these little noises that are either encouraging or discouraging depending on their tone, and I listen for them, adjusting as she needs.

I want her to know the truth…I will care for her.

On and on it goes, moving at this slow pace that is driving me mad with want. I can feel the tension building, my body dying to give her a few quick hard thrusts until I cum so hard, I go blind.

But I don't. And I'm rewarded when her hips finally rise up to meet mine. That's the moment I know…she's enjoying it too.

And that's all I need to keep the pace slow, to hold it steady as her body adjusts and then…enjoys.

It was the worth the wait.

One of her legs wraps around me, even as her pussy tightens on my cock, her breathy cry in my ear making my teeth grit as I squeeze my eyes shut. So good.

I pick up the tempo the slightest bit, my pelvic bone pushing against her clit in a way that has her crying out again and I know she's getting close.

I'm shaking with the effort to last. But as much as I want the orgasm, I want hers more.

Her breathy cries fill my ears as she becomes so tight, she's like a vice around my cock and I feel myself slipping, the orgasm overpowering my control.

A guttural cry rips from my throat and I'm cumming like I never have before. Like my insides are being turned out. It doesn't sound good, but it feels amazing.

Charlotte lets out a long moan and then she breaks apart, her body shaking as we orgasm together, the moment so much more than I ever imagined it would be.

She sinks into the bed, and I sink on top of her, finding her mouth and kissing her over and over.

Her fingers slide down my back and then back up my neck, brushing the new set of scratches on my skin.

I feel the tug of pain and smile against her mouth. We both like a little bit of pain mixed in with our pleasure.

I hook her waist, settling her deeper into the bed as I wrap my body around hers.

I thread our fingers together and look at the ring nestled on her finger. "Are you wearing the sapphire too?"

She pulls her other hand out from under her, turning it so I can see the ring. Her eyes are closed but there is a small smile on her face. "I'll miss them."

My brow draws together as I study her face. She doesn't look sad, maybe just wistful. Where does she think she's going? Clearly, I haven't been clear enough. "I don't see why you would."

She looks back at me, her sleepy eyes blinking. "What does that mean?"

"They are yours," I answer, kissing her shoulder. "Everything I've given you is yours." *Even me. I'm yours too.*

Something keeps me from saying the words out loud. She keeps talking about when she leaves...

I know I'll fight for her to stay, but I don't need to fight yet. She still needs me to keep her safe and I've got until this all ends to feel her out, decide upon the words, and share my feelings. It's new for me and I'm still finding my way.

"Mason," she whispers. "You can't give these to me. They must have cost—"

"Princess," I push up on one elbow, my fingers sliding down her arm. "Nobody tells me what I can and can't buy. That's one of the perks of being me."

A half smile tilts a corner of her mouth up. Her camera is still sitting on my nightstand and she reaches for it, lifting it up and turning it around.

"You're going to take a selfie with a digital SLR?"

"Watch me," she says as snaps several photos, lifting up a bit to kiss my cheek as the flash goes off again.

I look down at her, holding her gaze for a moment, the flash continuing to fill the room before I kiss her mouth. She's taken several more pictures, but I've gotten used to her obsession with photography and I stopped worrying she'd share them days ago. Charlotte excels at privacy.

And if I'm honest, I love the pictures. Every one is beautiful, made even more so because they are us.

She stretches out to set the camera on the nightstand again, and I lean with her to kiss her spine at the small of her back.

Her hand reaches around me, stroking my ribs before she turns back to me.

She settles into my embrace, her eyes closing again, a sigh spills from her lips. "You really know how to wear a girl out."

"Damn right I do," I answer even as I pull the covers tighter over her body.

I feel her relaxing into sleep when from the kitchen, her phone chimes. And then it chimes again.

"Is that the phone I gave you?"

"Mmhmm," she answers, her eyes remaining closed.

"Charlotte?"

"No," she rouses a bit. "It's my old phone."

"Who would be texting you at this time of night?" Worry has me tensing, pushing up onto my elbow.

She looks at the clock. "Probably Kim. Her shift just ended. She said Gus has her working doubles."

I relax back into the bed as I hear the phone a third time. "Insistent."

"She's pissed that she hasn't heard from me in days. And I can't exactly explain…"

That's Charlotte. Discreet. I kiss her shoulder, wondering how one person could be so perfect for me.

"Call her tomorrow. You can tell her my name. I'm about to turn up the heat on anyone who might think about hurting you."

Her legs tangle in mine. "Do I say we're engaged?"

"Yes," I answer, gathering her closer. "And then quit Rebel's. You won't be going back there."

"I'd object to your bossiness but I agree," she snuggles her face into my shoulder.

I smile again, brushing her hair back from her cheek as my fingers skim the velvet of her skin. "You love my bossiness."

I can see she's almost asleep, but I can't get enough of her skin. I could make love to her again and again.

I'm not sure I'll ever get enough.

"I loved your spanking."

My cock goes instantly hard as I comb my fingers through her hair. But I don't get a chance to answer as she drifts off to sleep.

Settling myself down, I hear the phone chime a fourth time.

For a friend who has been quiet, Kim is insistent tonight. I'll have to have Kim over for dinner, so she stops worrying. Charlotte is important to me and that means so is Kim.

My eyes close too. It was a day.

But tomorrow, tomorrow was going to be better. At least that is the hope…

CHAPTER TWENTY-FIVE

CHARLOTTE

I'M asleep when I hear the ring of a phone. Jerking awake, I realize two facts simultaneously. One, it's late, the sun is streaming into the windows.

And two...Mason is still in bed with me. We haven't slept past seven in the morning with the exception of that first night when we'd not gone to bed until about five.

I look at the clock realizing it's already nine.

Mason rolls over, picking up the phone. "'Lo?"

I turn toward him and he's instantly settling me close again, his arm draped around my back, his hand possessively placed on my hip.

"Are you still asleep?" Roman. I can hear him on the other end, which makes sense. My ear is less than a foot from the phone.

"Not anymore," Mason rumbles.

"If you're expecting me to apologize, I'm not going to. While you've been in bed, I've been working."

Mason's fingers stroke my hip and then slide up my side as he drops several kisses into my hair.

I'm not sure what I expected from this arrangement with Mason, but I didn't realize there would be so much snuggling. It's an unexpected perk, I think as I stretch, rolling onto my back as my hands rise up above my head.

Roman is still complaining as Mason runs his large palm over my stomach, leaning down to suck on one of my nipples. I gasp, not considering he'd do that while on the phone with his brother.

Roman stops talking. "What the fuck was that?"

"Charlotte just woke up," he answers, nonplussed. In fact, he's grinning like a cat who just drank the milk. "If you don't want to apologize to me, maybe you want to say sorry to her."

"Mason. After your round of calls last night, where you instilled the fear of God into the other families, they have all gotten back to me. We're having the all-family meeting tonight."

I feel the change in Mason. He stiffens, his face going hard as he sits up in bed. His attention has been completely diverted and I try not to wince. "Tonight?"

He's trying to keep me safe. He's a billionaire businessman. And this is a temporary arrangement. I repeat the list like a mantra, trying to keep my head straight.

Still, I lean forward, brushing my lips across his bare shoulder. He reaches back, wrapping his arm around my body and I do the same, my hand on his chest.

"Nine. We need to prepare, all be on the same page. But there is more."

"What?"

"Leo was spotted last night. He slipped our men, but it was him." Relief makes me melt into Mason. As much as he said Leo's antics were not my fault, I still felt responsible.

"Where?" Mason lets me go, sliding from the bed and walking into the bathroom so that I don't hear the rest of the conversation.

I flop back down on the bed, trying to control the insecurities. I gave Mason my virginity. Another bucket list item, one of two I promised myself I'd complete.

But now that that is done. What is next? Mason swears I'm getting out of this and that he'll keep me safe forever. I trust him to keep his word. Which means I need a plan. Will Kim and I still go to New York? Will I see Mason sometimes? My throat closes.

I want to take pictures for the rest of my life. But I don't care about marketing the same way I do about the art.

I pick up my camera and look at the pictures I'd taken last night. Some of them steal my breath.

The look in Mason's eye right before he kisses me...

It's enough to melt the panties right off any normal woman. And the picture of our kiss? I'm sending them all to the printer before I've even thought about it.

Then, setting down the camera, I head into my bathroom and start my shower. I'm nearly done when Mason appears.

It's a good thing he has large showers because he's made a habit of joining me. But this morning, I'm especially glad to see him. I feel even more vulnerable after last night and as he steps in, I move over, grabbing the soap in my hand.

"Everything all right?" I ask as I start soaping his back.

"It's good," he says with a smile over his shoulder. "Just a big day. But by tomorrow, the worst of this will hopefully be behind us."

I kiss his shoulder again as I keep soaping lower, my hands coming to his front. I'm sliding lower, wanting the closeness only intimacy can provide.

But he grabs my hands, stopping me before I've gotten too far, giving them a squeeze before he gently pulls them away. Another wave of disappointment hits me, though I try to ignore it. He just said he had an intense day. He needs his space.

Which is why I get out of the shower and towel off, tipping my head upside down to dry my hair.

"Woman," he growls as the water turns off. "Don't tease me like that."

I giggle, some part of me relieved. I'd worried that after I gave him my virginity, his protection and his affection would end.

I flip my head up and turn to face him naked, leaning back against the counter. "Who's teasing?"

He puts his hands on the counter on either side of me, capturing my mouth with his. "When I get home tonight, we are going to celebrate."

"You'll be careful today, won't you?"

"These are public meetings. Don't worry."

"They did try to blow us up," I answer, as I place my hands on his chest.

"They'll retaliate for sure when they learn I'm tightening the vise. That's why it's important you stay out of sight. Promise me."

I nod as he pushes off the counter.

"With that said, I know I mentioned that you could tell Kim my name. Why don't you invite her here? I can send Jackson for her. You and Kim could spend some time together."

"I'm allowed guests?" I ask as we both make our way into my room.

"You're not a prisoner." He kisses me again. "Any chance you could put out breakfast while I dress?"

"Of course," I answer as I slip into a simple dress. My hair and makeup can wait. I'm busy in the kitchen as I cook a few eggs, and I realize I'm also famished.

Mason comes out dressed, wolfs down his breakfast, and then drops a kiss on my forehead before he heads for the door. "We're having all the meetings today down on the second floor of this building."

"Here?" I turn to look at him as I take a bite of my own breakfast.

"I'm not going to be further away than a few floors if you need me."

"Thank you," I say as I watch him go. Is he staying in the building for my benefit? I swallow down a lump as I finish my breakfast and then start getting ready for the day. Once I've blown out my hair, I pull the pictures from the printer, adding them to the book I'm creating for Mason.

Sitting on the couch, I spread my project out on the coffee table, adding pictures here, rearranging them there. I'm creating a story with them, only I don't actually know the ending.

I've done all the pictures in black and white and the whole series is an ode to Mason. It begins as fractured pieces, just small shots of his hand or his arm, and builds to fuller, whole pictures, and finally the emotional images from last night.

It feels like some sort of culmination, and I suppose it is.

I've given Mason my virginity and my heart. But I started taking these pictures to answer the question of his intentions.

I start from the beginning. The images are beautiful but cold.

As I move along, they warm. Is that my feelings or his? I stop on the one from last night where he looks at me before he kisses me.

What do I see in his eyes? Possessiveness, but that's always been there. Tenderness too. It's in the way his hand is wrapped about my back. He's not grabbing my ass, he's supporting my weight.

And the kiss, it's hot and yet it's gentle. More gentle than I ever imagined from him. Blood is rushing in my ears. Am I imagining it or does Mason have some feelings for me too?

He told me he'd protect me forever. Maybe, I'm not...

My phone dings again and I leave the photo book to pick it up.

It's Kim.

HEY YOU, you promised to call. Where are you?

BUT MY BROW WRINKLES. It's the only message from her. There are none from last night and I click back out of my chat with her and look at the list of messages.

I gasp, nearly dropping my phone. My late-night messages were not from Kim.

They were from Leo.

Of course he had my number when we dated. I never changed it, but I also would have thought he'd have deleted me from his contacts a long time ago...

. . .

My hand trembling, I touch the messages, my eyes flying over the words.

I know you think you're all cozy in that penthouse with Mason as your big bad protector.

But you should know that he promised the entire family that he'd give you to the Dukes to punish the Italians. Did he tell you that while he tucked you in his bed?

He never cared about you. You have always been a means to an end.

Like I said. You chose the wrong brother.

I don't even realize I've sunk to the floor until my hand presses to the tile.

My eyes have blurred so I can't even read the messages again. Is it true? Was I always just a pawn in Mason's plot for revenge?

Did he plan to turn me over? I've been wondering why he'd go to such lengths and now I feel like I have the piece of the puzzle I was always missing. It all makes sense.

I shake my head, carefully setting my phone next to me on the floor. My head spins as I try to get up. What a stupid fool I was…

Drawing in a deep breath, I try to come up with a plan…

Picking up my other phone, I call down to Jackson.

"Hey, Charlotte," he says, his voice friendly as ever.

"Hey, Jackson," I reply as I clear my throat, I can hear the emotion in my vocal cords, but I try to shake them off. I don't want Jackson to worry. I don't even have a super clear plan here. I just need to get out. Find some space and think…

"Everything all right?" Jackson asks in his usual friendly way.

"Fine. I just need to go out to the store. I—"

"Sorry, Charlotte. No can do."

"What?" I can barely breathe my pulse is racing so quickly.

"Mason's orders. No one can come in or out."

My fingers touch my forehead. "I thought I wasn't a prisoner," I whisper as much to myself as to him. But he still hears me.

"Rules apply to everyone, even me," Jackson answers. "With the bombing, everyone is staying in the building, using the empty apartments. Safer."

I shake my head. How am I going to face Mason after reading those texts? "I need to leave, Jackson. I can't stay I..." My voice breaks.

"Hang on. What's got you so—" But his voice cuts out as I hear a thump and then another, the sound of the phone clattering on the ground, creating static on the line.

"Jackson? Jackson?" I call into the phone. But I hear a click and then the phone line goes dead.

I stare at my phone wondering what is going on when the light to the elevator illuminates.

For a second I blink at it, trying to puzzle out what's happening. Who could be coming up? No one has the code but family...

And then my brain starts to work. Someone knocked Jackson out. Took his phone. The phone with the code. But who?

But I don't wait for the answer as I grab my phone and run...

CHAPTER TWENTY-SIX

CHARLOTTE

THERE AREN'T many places to hide in Mason's penthouse, even his bed has a frame that goes to the floor, so I end up in the cabinet in his bathroom.

With shaking fingers, I turn my ringer off and then dial Mason.

It rings twenty times before it goes to voicemail, a half sob fills my chest but I push it down and try again.

My heart is pounding in my chest as the phone goes to voicemail a second time.

That's when I hear the ding of the elevator.

I stifle a scream as the sound of footsteps on the marble floor echo through the apartment.

"Charlotte."

My breath catches as I try to dial again. My vision is blurring but I know who the voice belongs to. Leo. I don't answer. I'm not helping him find my hiding spot.

"What are you doing, Charlotte? Come on out, sweetheart. We need to talk."

Sweetheart. I am not his sweetheart. I'm not Mason's either if what Leo has said is true.

I hit the call button again, the line ringing for a third time.

Finally, he picks up. "Charlotte?"

"Mason," I whisper in a quick rush. "Hurry. Leo's here."

"Fuck." He doesn't hang up, but he doesn't say anything else as his footsteps echo through the line.

I've got the phone to my ear when Leo calls again, the sound closer. "Where are you? I'm guessing we don't have a lot of time for hide and seek, so why don't you come out so we can have a little chat."

I don't say a word, but the smallest whimper escapes my lips.

Mason snarls into the phone his steps moving quicker as Leo enters the bathroom.

"I know you read my texts, Charlotte. I saw the moment you saw them. You have to turn off the *Read* feature but then again, you've always been crap with technology."

I shrink deeper into the cabinet.

"So I know you know that Mason was always going to betray you."

"Fuck," Mason grunts into the phone. Clearly he can hear Leo too. "That motherfucker."

"Come with me and we'll go far away," Leo says standing just above the cabinet. He knows I'm here. "Mexico? South of France?"

I'm shaking, barely able to hold the phone. I don't trust Mason in this moment, but I trust Leo way less...

I know I shouldn't trust Mason, but right now, I just want him here.

The door opens and Leo's face appears. I scream then and Mason snarls into my ear as Leo grins. "Who are you talking to?"

"Put my fucking brother on the phone," Mason rumbles into the line through gritted teeth.

I hold out the phone to Leo, our eyes locked, though I'm still completely silent.

Leo takes it, his fingers brushing mine. It takes everything in me not to recoil. "Hello, big brother."

"Touch one hair on her head—"

"Don't play that shit," Leo spits back. "She knows the truth, Mason. Knows how you told the entire family you'd hand her over to the Dukes. Enjoy your tunnel and your money."

And then Leo throws my phone, grabbing my arm with a quick jerk. Burning pain shoots through me as he wrenches my shoulder socket.

I scream again, as I land half out of the cabinet. The small of my back landing awkwardly on the lip of the cabinet and more pain shoots through me.

Leo wraps an arm around my waist pulling me the rest of the way out. "Stop fighting, Charlotte, and you won't get hurt."

"Let me go," I cry, trying to pull away, trying to fight. With his hands on my waist, he hauls me over his shoulder, my fight doing almost nothing to stop him. "Please, Leo. Please let me go."

"I'm doing this for your own good."

I sob out a gasping cry as my good hand fists and pounds on his back. "This is not for my good."

I think I hear Mason roar through my phone on the other side of the room, but I can't be sure as I try to kick my legs.

"You want to stay here and let him turn you over to the Dukes? Don't be stupid, Charlotte."

"I don't want to go with you!" I cry, squirming, which only makes his arm tighten.

"I know you don't. I saw that book you made, stupid woman." He smacks my ass, making me go still. It's not like when Mason does it. It's meant to humiliate, not excite, and I try to hit him back, though I'm like a buzzing fly. I'm just annoying him. "But try to understand you are safer with me than you ever were with him."

"It's not true."

"Mason doesn't get to win this one," he roars, his strides growing longer.

He's carrying me away from the bathroom and my phone. I give a desperate sob. "Please put me down, Leo. You're scaring me."

"You won't be scared when we're sitting on a beach."

"You hurt my shoulder," I try again. Just trying to say something, anything to make him stop. Delay. "I can't feel my arm."

He pauses at those words, stopping in the hall. His shoulders are even larger than Mason's, the rough edge cutting into my belly. "We'll look at it later. I know Mason's already en route. We don't have much time. The drive—"

"He's not driving," I shake my head, realizing that Leo has made a miscalculation. He thinks Mason is at the Kincaid Enterprise building and not here.

The elevator whirs and though I can't see the light…I know. Mason is on his way. Relief makes me limp against Leo's back.

"Who is that?"

I don't answer. I don't need to. We don't move as I hear the elevator doors open.

"What the fuck do you think you're doing?" Mason spits and I hiccup a cry knowing that Leo isn't taking me anywhere. My eyes fill with tears but upside down, they just rest on my lashes. "Put her down."

I hear the click of a gun, the hammer cocking back, and I stiffen again, trying to lift up.

"Don't move, Charlotte," Mason commands as he crosses the room. I go still again.

"Such a good girl, isn't she, big brother?" Leo says as he gently sets my feet on the floor. The blood has rushed to my head and I sway as his hands leave me. "And completely smitten with you. You win again, don't you?"

Leo raises his hands up.

"It was never a competition." Mason reaches me, turning me and pulling me against him. He catches my shoulder and I suck in my breath as pain shoots through my arm.

Mason's gaze flicks down me, assessing the damage, before he tucks me behind him.

"You're right about that," Leo straightens his shoulders. "Charlotte has been yours since our second date. The company yours. The family yours. The revenge yours."

I press myself to Mason's back, useless tears leaking from my eyes.

Next to me, Roman appears, a pistol in his hand. Jake comes to my other side and I hear Luke step up behind me. I'm surrounded but not entirely certain I'm safe. Is Mason going to hand me over tonight?

Has this all been a ploy to keep me here?

"Leo," Mason says in a flat voice. "It's not—"

"It's all right, big brother. You're right not to trust me. My move against the Italians got this place bombed, didn't it? But you, man who thinks of everything, saw that possibility. Built this place to withstand it."

I feel Mason stiffen. "Your move against the Italians? You'd better explain."

CHAPTER TWENTY-SEVEN

MASON

I'M GOING to kill my brother.

All right, maybe I'm not going to actually murder him, but I'm seriously tempted.

Charlotte is trembling against my back, the screams she'd let out had turned my blood ice cold. The feeling that she's mine to protect has been swelling for a while, building into this near unstoppable force.

No man is going to touch her ever again. And Leo is going to answer to me.

"Explain?" Leo says, scratching his chin. "I'll start with the fact that I created a giant calling card that had Vendetti frothing to end me."

All those incidents at the casinos, the last one being the Italians. Leo knew that the Italian hit men would be waiting for him. "Go on."

But Leo shakes his head. "You first."

"Me first what?" I ask, reaching an arm behind me to gently wrap around Charlotte. She needs to know she's safe.

One of her hands flattens out on my back, her cheek pressed between my shoulder blades.

Leo gives me a cold smile. "Your confession first."

My lip curls. "And what is it you think I need to confess?"

"How you promised all of us that you'd sacrifice Charlotte to our new competitors if it meant you got your revenge. Come on, man with a plan, tell Charlotte how she was just another tool for you to use."

I feel the shiver that runs through her, the soft rush of her breath. "Leo."

"She's in love with you, you know," Leo practically snarls. "And I think she ought to know the sort of man she wants to give her heart too."

"How would you even know how she feels? How I feel?" I ask, my chest growing tight. Charlotte tries to push away from me, but I keep her in place with a very light pressure. She's safest pressed to my back.

"She made you a book," Leo shakes his head. "I've got to hand it to you, Mason. You are a winner." He points a finger at me. "I wanted to get Vendetti to prove to this family that I'm a winner too. And I will succeed. It's practically done."

"And trying to take Charlotte against her will. Does that make you a winner too?"

"Can't blame a guy for wanting to take you down a peg or two." He smiles again. "I'll tell you the rest after you tell Charlotte the truth."

My heart is slowing as I spread out my fingers, trying to keep her close. "I did not say I'd sacrifice Charlotte for revenge." I know I'm trying to find a loophole here.

"What did you say you'd sacrifice her for then? For what reason would you give her over to the Dukes?"

I feel a shudder run through her as my own temperature drops. I've promised Charlotte protection, but how will she trust me to keep her safe when she hears this.

Maybe she shouldn't, except everything is different now and I'm not sure how to say that. I haven't even told her how I feel about her.

I've armed Leo with this information and he's going to use it to drive a wedge between me and her. I seriously doubt I'm winning this one. Not with her.

I feel my heart cracking as Charlotte's soft sobs fill my ears.

I turn my back to my brother, wrapping my arms around her. Her face is too pale, it's almost chalk white. "Take Leo downstairs. We'll finish this conversation—"

"We'll finish it here," Charlotte speaks for the first time since I heard her on the phone. Her voice is barely a whisper but it's resolute. "We'll finish it now." She notches her chin.

"Charlotte," Roman says. "Don't listen to Leo. He's not trying to help you, he's—"

"I know what he's doing," Charlotte says as she steps to the side. That's when I notice that her arm is hanging at an odd angle. Red blurs my vision.

"What's wrong with your arm?"

She barely looks at me. "I don't know."

"How did that fucking happen?" It's a snarl of words as I look back at Leo with my fists locked into two anvils.

"Leo—"

But she only gets out the name when I spin and in a single motion land a fist right in Leo's nose. Blood spurts from the wound as Leo takes three steps back but I'm on him before he can recover, hitting him several more times.

"Mason!" Charlotte screams. "Stop."

I do, taking three steps back but my hands are still clenched at my sides, my feet in a wide stance. "He hurt you. I'm going to do far worse than break his nose."

She steps between me and him as she turns to Leo, his face mangled from the blows I've landed, blood streaming down his chin. "You've made your point, Leo," she says quietly. "But I have one to make too. One I should have said two years ago."

She draws in a deep breath as she moves to the counter and, one-handed, gets a wad of paper towels, handing it to Leo.

He holds it against his nose. "What's that?"

She shakes her head. "I was trying to find a way to end things that night at the club."

Leo drops the paper towels staring at her as his lip curls. "You think I don't know that? I'm aware you chose him from the moment you met him."

She shakes her head. "If you're aware, why were you trying to get me to run away with you?"

"Because…" Leo presses the paper towels to his nose again. "Of all the men in my family, I'm the fuck-up who is exactly like my dad. Everyone knows it. Even you." His eyes close. "You understood from the second date, didn't you?"

A moment ago, I hated my brother, but those words make something soften. I can understand feeling like I was going to fall into the same trap our father had, that I was cut from the same cloth.

It's been tearing him up inside just like it was me.

Charlotte shakes her head. "I don't know anything about your father, Leo, but I do know you're not going to get very far fighting against your family. Going it alone is a point of great weakness. Trust me on that."

Leo's shoulders droop. "I'm getting advice from you now?"

She turns to me then, and my stomach drops. I can see her face hardening.

"Charlotte," it comes out like I'm begging. I am.

She shakes her head. "I don't want to hear whatever Leo wanted you to say, but I don't think I can stay here either."

I glare at Leo, any understanding or sympathy gone. "You can't leave. I told you, if I do one thing it will be to keep you safe."

"I can't stay with you," her breath catches, pain pulling at the lines of her face. "I was only ever…" She grimaces in pain.

I step closer, reaching out a hand, but she winces away.

"She can come stay in the apartment with me and Luke. She'll still be in the building," Roman offers. He's dropped the pistol, but he's still giving Leo a hard glare.

"And me? Where am I going with the all-families meeting set for tonight?" Leo asks.

"Know about that, do you?" I ask, my fingers itching to pull Charlotte close. She's drooping, I can see her back curling, her body weakening. I reach for her, but she steps to the side, avoiding my touch. Apparently, she still has energy for that.

"Roman," I say, my voice hoarse. "Take Charlotte to the couch. She's in pain."

"I'll call the doctor."

"What are you going to tell him?" Jake asks. "There's a woman surrounded by four men with a broken shoulder?"

"Broken," I growl out, losing my focus once again.

"More likely dislocated," Roman offers as he takes her hand and brings her over to the couch. "I've seen it before."

She sits, wilting to the side. "I'll tell him we were practicing for our wedding dance," she says closing her eyes. "I just want it fixed."

The other men nod, but I'm not satisfied. Not even a little. "I would never hurt—"

"You'd just give me to your competitors." Her tone is so bitter, I'm taken aback.

But Roman is looking down at something on the coffee table before he looks up at me. There's a message in his eyes I don't understand.

"Leo can go with Jake, who will keep an eye on him." Roman punches some numbers into his phone. "And I know a doctor who is discreet."

"I'm going with Jake?" Leo grunts. "Are you taking me out to the desert, Uncle Jake? Is that how this ends?"

Jake doesn't answer, he's looking at Charlotte too. "You know something? I like her. I don't say that about many women." And then he steps close to me. "Make it right."

I shake my head. Jake is the last person I expected to hear words like that from. "Jake?"

"Roman might have had a point. We could use a bit of softness around here, and I can't deny that she's got the right temperament for our work." And then he pulls out a cigar, lighting it in my apartment. "But I think you're going to need to grovel."

Grovel? Is that even going to be enough?

CHAPTER TWENTY-EIGHT

Mason

The doctor arrives and it's a good thing he's discreet. We've brought Jackson up from the garage, with a nasty cut on his head, Leo is still bleeding from the nose, and Charlotte has gone from pale to ashen.

I've seen brawls with less injuries.

And all of this before we have a meeting with all four families. A meeting where I need every bit of confidence and power, and inside I'm dying as I watch Charlotte suffer.

That feeling that I might rip my brother to shreds fills my chest again. She's slumped on the couch, her features in a perpetual wince.

I walk over to her as the doctor looks at her shoulder. Not one to cause a scene, she lets me take her hand in mine. "You all right, baby?"

"I'm…" Her features pull even tighter. "It really hurts."

I bring her hand to my lips, kissing it as the doctor finishes the examination. "It's dislocated. I'm going to have put it back into place."

My teeth grind together as my lips thin. I hate the thought of her being in pain. It makes me crazy, and I don't even realize I'm cursing until everyone turns to look at me. Even Charlotte.

"Mason."

"I wish it was me," I whisper, touching her cheek.

She gives me a small smile and hope fills my chest.

"You can hold her nice and still for me while I put it back into place. If we were in the hospital, I would give her an anesthetic." The doctor frowns, looking at the other injured men. I know he's wondering... "But it will be less painful for her to have me pop it back in now than to wait."

"Can I hold you, sweetheart?" I feel my family looking at me, I don't care. I know they've never seen this side of me. Hell. I barely recognized this man. But Charlotte deserves all the tenderness I am capable of giving. And more, if I'm being honest.

Tentatively, she nods.

"I think the bedroom would be best," the doctor clears his throat. "I'll put it back in place while she's lying flat on her back. How firm is your mattress?"

"Not very," I answer, my brow crinkling.

"Maybe the island then."

"Is it going to hurt?" Charlotte asks, her voice barely above a whisper.

"Yes," the doctor answers and my fist balls into my thigh. "But then, you're going to feel better. I know how painful a dislocated shoulder is."

I help Charlotte stand, trying not to hurt her more than she already hurts. We make our way to the counter while Jake gets a pillow. I have to lift her in my arms to get her on the counter and she whimpers softly as I lay her down.

Jake slides the pillow under her head, his eyes filled with a tension he doesn't usually display.

I place my chest on her chest, holding her head between my hands. "It's all right, sweetheart. It's going to be better soon. I promise."

She looks at me, pain and worry brimming in her eyes as the doctor extends out her arm. "I'm going to give a quick pull to put the joint back in the socket."

Her eyes squeeze shut as I hold her still.

I see the doctor tug at the exact moment she screams, the sound cutting through me as I drop my forehead to hers.

But her eyes don't open. I jerk my face back, studying her, waiting for her eyes to meet mine. "Charlotte?" I can hear the fear in my voice, my hands tightening on the back of her head, but she's completely limp in my hands. "Sweetheart?" Raw panic, has me giving her a small shake.

"She fainted from the pain," the doctor says in this matter-of-fact voice that makes me want to hit things.

The doctor…maybe.

Leo. Definitely. I look up to see him still holding a wadded-up ball of bloody paper towels to his nose, his eyes wide. "Is she all right?" he asks when his gaze meets mine.

I snarl in response, ready to go another round. Maybe ten. He did this to her. And I'd go make him suffer but I can't drag myself away from Charlotte.

I look back down at her, fear swelling in my chest. I need her to wake up. "Princess." The nickname comes out in a broken whisper.

"Call her queen," Roman says from the other side of the counter. "She's earned it."

The doctor comes back over, waving smelling salts under her nose and her eyes jerk open.

Relief makes me limp as the doctor sets some pills on the counter. "For the pain. I'll give you a sling as well to keep the arm immobile. She should be seen by a surgeon to make sure she doesn't need surgery."

And then, he moves to Jackson, tending the cut on the old guy's head.

But I barely pay attention as my gaze holds Charlotte's. My thumbs are stroking over her cheeks, and I press several small kisses to her forehead. She's still limp in my arms.

"I'm all right, Mason. It's better now."

My gaze slashes to Leo again, who has the decency to look pained. That scream was like nails on a chalkboard. And as much as I want to care for her in this moment, I'm aware that I am the source of her pain.

It's my relationship with my brother that brought all this about.

The doctor is talking to Roman about Jackson's care, as I look at Jake. "The doctor is going to give you instructions about Leo."

Jake scowls. "Will his instructions involve how to break his fucking arm? Because I don't think his nose is enough."

Leo lets out a long breath. "I fucked that one up, I get it. I should have never tried to pull Charlotte from that cabinet."

"That's what you're apologizing for?" My teeth are gritted and it's only the doctor's presence that keeps me from saying more. He might be discreet, but I don't trust anyone that is not part of this family.

But Leo's not done. "And when did my entire family join the Charlotte camp?"

Jake's gaze catches mine, his brows lifting. "When Mason decided to marry her."

Charlotte starts, her muscles gaining some rigidity. "We're not getting married."

"I know you're angry with me," I start, wanting some privacy with Charlotte. I'm not even sure I'm going to that meeting tonight. All I care about is holding her in my arms. None of my other plans matter.

In fact, leaving Las Vegas and this whole mess behind us is starting to sound like a good idea. Charlotte and I can go somewhere far away. I'll start a new business. Just as long as she is by my side.

"I am." Her eyes go hard with the words as my stomach sinks.

"I know I fucked up—"

"You did."

"Is this about forgiveness, then? Apologies? Explanations? Whatever you need..." I'm still holding her head in my hands as I start massaging small circles on her cheeks. I'll grovel. I'll beg. I just need her to listen.

"Yes... but also..." She's relaxing back in my hands. "You haven't actually asked yet."

A smile curls my lips before I bend down and gently kiss her. "Is now too soon?"

"Yes."

I shake my head. It's time I started making some promises. "I know you want to leave Vegas. I'll go with you. Anywhere you want..." Jake is hearing all of this, but I don't care. He and Roman can take over. "We'll start over."

Charlotte shakes her head. "Running away is my thing. Remember? Not yours."

"I suppose that's true."

"I'm not running this time." She touches my cheek with her uninjured hand. "And I might be willing to forgive, but you have to meet me halfway."

"Anything," I whisper. Watching her suffer has made me even more certain that I am supposed to be her protector. I love this woman. I think I have for a long time.

She looks over at Leo. "You need to forgive your brother."

"No." That is one thing I'm not willing to give.

CHAPTER TWENTY-NINE

CHARLOTTE

MASON'S GLARE at Leo would turn a lesser man to dust.

Leo, however, bleeding nose and all, just glares back. They are so alike in this way. And that swagger is what made me interested in Leo for a hot minute.

But he's different than Mason too in ways that would never suit me. He's impulsive, hot-tempered.

It's Mason's methodical control that keeps me from running scared. My fingers flex against Mason's cheek. "I know if you really think this through, like you always do, you'll know I'm right."

He drops his face to mine, kissing the tip of my nose, and then both my cheeks, his kiss so light and gentle, he's clearly worried he might break me.

"He's going to need time, Charlotte," Leo interjects. "He's been angry at me for a while for being so like our father."

Mason sits up straighter. "I'm not angry at you for that."

"Yes, you are." Leo's voice gets harder too.

"I'm not."

"Then why don't you give me more responsibility?"

"Because..." Mason rumbles in frustration. "Your method of solving problems resulted in all of this..." He sweeps his hand around the room.

Leo winces. "Only because I was trying to prove myself to you."

The doctor steps up to examine Leo's nose and Mason and his brother stop talking. Instead, Mason looks down at me, his face softening. He reaches for the sling, helping me put it on my injured arm and then he helps me up from the hard counter to return to the couch. The shoulder still throbs and aches and once I'm settled on the couch, he gets a glass of water and one of the pills the doctor gave me.

I swallow it down, lounging back. I'd been about to run but between my shoulder, and Mason's public affection, I know I'm not going anywhere. For once in my life, I'm going to stay right here and I'm going to ask Mason some of the hard questions.

How does he feel about me? What does he see in our future? It's time for me to be a big girl.

But as he sits down next to me, settling my legs over his lap, his hand skates up my hip, settling on my waist. "Charlotte?"

"Yes?" I steel myself for whatever comes next because I know we're about to really start talking. I want this, but my stomach still clenches.

"I'm in love with you." His eyes are steady and strong as he stares at me and my heart jumps into my throat as the air rushes from my lungs.

"I'm in love with you too." I can't hold back the words, and even if I could, everyone in this room knows it's true.

"I want you to marry me."

"Is that how you ask?" I know I'm playing a bit hard to get, but he deserves it. Still, my lips curl into a small smile.

"I did already buy a ring."

I shake my head. I know I'll say yes...eventually. I want to be part of Mason's family, in part because Jake was right. It needs a bit of softening and that involves a little forgiveness and grace.

Mason picks up my book from the coffee table and flips to the beginning. He turns the pages, his expression stoic and difficult to read so I don't try. Instead, I close my eyes, the medication starting to take effect.

The pain is diminishing, but it's also making me sleepy.

I must drift off and I don't wake until he brushes his fingers down my exposed leg. "When did you make this?"

"I finished it this morning before I got Leo's texts."

"And how long have you known how you felt…about me?"

"I don't know," I try to open my eyes, but my lids are so heavy. "Maybe always."

"How long is she going to be asleep?"

I don't hear the doctor's answer. In fact, I don't hear anything for a while.

I wake up a few times, all the men still there, but seated around the table. I have no idea how much time has passed. "Mason?"

He gets up immediately, leaving the conversation and bringing me a glass of water. Holding my head, he brings the glass to my lips.

Once I'm done drinking, he brushes my hair back. "Hungry?"

"Still tired."

"Go back to sleep, sweetheart." He kisses my forehead. "I'll be here when you wake."

"But what about your meeting?"

"You're more important than any meeting."

I blink in surprise. This is *the* meeting. The one he's been waiting for where he keeps us all safe by making sure the other families fall in line. "But…"

"I'll explain later. Go back to sleep."

And then he kisses me again. I don't mean to, but I do fall back to sleep, and I don't wake again until the sun is setting in the Las Vegas sky.

The others have left, but Mason is still there, sitting across from me in one of the armchairs by the windows. "Mason?"

"You're awake."

"How long have I been asleep?"

He pushes out of the chair, coming to bend over me on the couch. "Eight hours at least. How is your arm?"

"It's sore," I say. My guess is it's black and blue, but I don't look now. "What time is it? What time is the meeting?"

"It starts soon." He strokes my cheek, resting on his haunches in front of me.

"You're going?"

His mouth twitches. "Roman can handle it."

I shake my head, wishing I could get up too. I'm so sore though, and my body feels really heavy. "You have to go."

"I need to take care of you."

"I'm here to make you stronger. Not weaker." I meet his gaze, hoping that he understands. I mean the words.

He leans forward, kissing my lips. "Is that what you're going to do?"

"I think so."

"See, I thought you were going to make certain I have a better work-life balance."

I laugh but that makes my arm hurt. "And Leo? How did you end things with him?"

Mason frowns. "He's sleeping in our bed, so clearly, I took your advice."

That makes me smile. "Really?"

"Really. Which means, when I ask you to marry me, I'm fully expecting you to say yes."

"Yes," I answer automatically, not even sure which question I'm answering.

He kisses me long and slow. The kind that makes me feel cherished. And then he's straightening up, heading to the fridge. He pulls out a takeout box, fixing me a plate.

"You need to eat."

"Bossy," I reply back, but the smell of the Thai food hits my nose, and my stomach gives a growl. I'm starving.

"Jackson is in the other bedroom. Do you need anything from in there? I'll get it for you. I have no idea how that crusty old bird sleeps. But we don't need you walking in and seeing any part of that."

"I'll be fine, Mason. Now go. Jackson and Leo are here if anything happens."

He grimaces. "You'd trust Leo?"

The truth is, I think Leo has learned his lesson where I'm concerned. Maybe he's learned a whole bunch of them. "I trust Jackson. And I assume you'll leave him with a few pistols."

Mason smiles but he sits down next to me. I start to slowly eat my noodles. He's clearly not in a rush as he starts playing with my hair. "You got it."

"It might be stressing me out that you haven't left."

"I know that this meeting is about our future, but I also understand that you are more important than any business venture." He leans closer. "My priorities have never been clearer."

I set down my chopsticks, looking at my fiancé. I do believe we are actually going to get married, and that is kind of crazy. "You're going to go because this meeting is really about keeping our family safe."

He looks at me for a long moment before he nods. "Well said, wife."

"Not yet I'm not," I answer but I know I'm smiling from his words.

"Soon." He winks as he pushes up from his seat and goes into first one bedroom and then the other.

Both Jackson and Leo emerge, Leo immediately helps himself to his own plate of noodles. He's got two black eyes to match his broken nose and I grin down into my noodles. I might have asked Mason to forgive Leo, but I'm not sorry that Leo probably hurts as much as I do.

Mason clears his throat. "I'm going to leave you all to eat. I need to—"

"I'm coming with you," Leo interrupts.

Mason shakes his head. "I don't think—"

"I don't have to say a word. I just want to see Toni's face." Leo holds up his hand. "And I'm done competing with you Mason. I concede. You lead. I follow."

"I appreciate that," Mason says, cocking his head. "But I'm curious. What great blow is Carcetti getting tonight?"

Leo smiles at his brother. "I want it to be a surprise. Consider it a wedding gift. But first, I will need a clean shirt."

"Fine," Mason answers, giving me a long-suffering look before he pivots toward the bedroom. "This is your fault, Charlotte."

"I'll never forgive myself," I answer with a giggle. Because I'm glad to see Mason and Leo getting along. This is how it should be.

Leo stops, looking between us. "You make a nice couple."

Mason starts for his room. "Hell has frozen over."

"Just wait...I've got an even bigger surprise for you tonight." Leo looks almost giddy now.

"Should I be worried?" Mason stops and I set down my noodles. I asked Mason to forgive Leo. I didn't make a mistake, did I?

"I don't think so." Leo shakes his head. "Though you might want to bring a weapon just in case. This is my brand of retribution, after all."

What had Leo done?

CHAPTER THIRTY

MASON

MY STOMACH IS as tight as a steel drum. Is it the meeting or the surprise Leo keeps referring to?

Leo and I take the elevator down to the second floor, quiet settling between us. "Want to tell me what I'm walking into?" I'm a man who likes a plan. Leo's surprise may be my downfall.

Leo quirks a shit grin. "Vendetti is in prison as of this morning."

I stop the elevator, turning to my brother. "You're serious? On the murder charge?"

"No. On the bombing." Leo scrubs a hand over the back of his neck. "He may or may not have had all the supplies for a pipe bomb in his trunk and someone might have filmed him setting off the bomb and sent that film to the police."

I stare at my brother. "You knew he was bombing us?"

"I did. And before you get mad, I also knew you built this building to withstand a much larger blast than that."

It wasn't the worst plan I'd ever heard. "And how did you know he'd attack?"

Leo grimaces. "I know my reputation. I pretended to be drunk, pretended to be mad at you and in a fake tirade, I may have let slip you had a witness here you weren't turning over."

"They know Charlotte?"

"No. Of course not. They don't even know the witness is female. But they'd also heard about the tunnel, and I think they were looking for an excuse to attack."

It wasn't the best plan, but it wasn't the worst either. I did not appreciate having my home attacked, but getting Vendetti into prison…that was a prize worth giving some skin for.

"And you think the Italians will still attend tonight?"

"They might because they now know you're calling in their debts." Leo jerks his chin toward the button. "Shall we? I know Jake has been waiting for this moment for a long time. If you really wanted Vendetti, he's got his sights set on Toni Carcetti."

This was information I already knew. Sitting around the table all afternoon, Jake had agreed to be the man who pressed the Italians. Roman would work with the Dukes, and Luke with the Russians.

Each group was going to either offer their allegiances or buy their way out of debt. There were no other options. Not that the Italians could ever pay enough…they were about to be squeezed out of this city after we put Toni in prison.

We had it all worked out. And tonight we would push the first domino when we called in the debts. I'd gather more favors from the families very soon. That was the thing about owning all the best real estate. When the tunnel was finished, my business, and that of my partners, would be booming.

I enter the makeshift conference room. I haven't told Charlotte yet, but this building is compromised in terms of its location, which means we'll be moving.

In the meantime, I'm having the meeting here because I don't want to be any more than a few floors from her at any moment.

Bringing everyone through the police tape to get here also helps set the right tone. I've been attacked. Retribution is coming…

But when we arrive late, it's obvious that the meeting is not off to a good start.

The Dukes sit on one side of the table, tall, polished, and distinguished with their classically good looks.

Across from them, the tattooed Bratva glare, looking rough and ready to break things.

But the Italians are not here....

"Motherfuckers didn't show." Jake spits as he stands, turning to me.

I shrug. They are making it too easy for me to gain the other families' allegiances. Toni Carcetti is going down.

Stopping at the head of the table, I smile at all the men who have collected. "I have an announcement to make."

Every man turns to look at me. Perhaps they think I'll mention the tunnel. Or maybe the bomb...

"I'm getting married." I raise my arms up, flashing a smile.

They give me a polite cheer and a clap as I step to the center of my family. "You can imagine the idea of starting a family has me craving a certain amount of stability."

Several men nod, though I can see them shift uncomfortably too. They know my measures might mean trouble for them. They're right. "And that's what I'm hoping you gentlemen can help me with."

It's time to begin...

CHAPTER THIRTY-ONE

CHARLOTTE

I FALL ASLEEP AGAIN, waiting for Mason to return. The sheets have been changed and the smell of crisp clean cotton makes it even harder to stay awake.

You'd think I'd be rested after sleeping the entire day, but I'm just exhausted.

I don't wake until Mason slips in the bed with me, his warm body pressing to mine. "How'd it go?"

"Excellent," is all he answers. "You and Jackson do all right?"

"Jackson and I did fine." I snuggle deeper into him, wishing that I could feel the slide of his skin against mine in some deeper way but I'm too sore.

Between losing my virginity last night, and now my shoulder, every part of my body aches.

"Are you going to tell me about the meeting?"

He smiles against my shoulder. "The Dukes are joining forces with us. They'll give us a percentage of their casino, and in return, I will connect my casino to theirs via the tunnel. They're on the cusp of buying another building and I artfully suggested they might consider waiting to see if the Italians go out of business and then they could have side-by-side properties. In addition, I've made it clear that their little incident, the one you witnessed, is best left forgotten by everyone. No one is saying anything, and everyone is happy."

I turn to look at him. He's done it…he's removed the threat to my life. "You're serious?"

He smiles. "About your safety? Very and always."

I wish I could turn to better face him, but I can't put any weight on my hurt shoulder at all. "And the Russians?"

"The Russians are lone wolves, which means they won't join with the Italians. They would like an opportunity to make me a business offer and I've given them a week to do so."

I shake my head. I sometimes forget that Mason is a man who can move mountains when he chooses.

"And the Italians?" His hand is tracing up and down my hip, his lips sliding over the back of my neck.

"They never showed, which means Jake is about to pay them a visit."

"Jake?"

"He and my father were best friends and brothers. He took the loss hard, and he's very motivated to see the Italians suffer." He places a light kiss on my hurt shoulder, his fingers skimming over the blooming bruises.

I look back at him. "Mason. Thank you…I don't know how to begin to tell you how much I appreciate—"

He kisses me, softly cupping my chin in his hand. "I appreciate your appreciation, but I need you to understand that my world has reordered and you are at the very top of my priorities. It is my first and most important job to keep you safe, my queen."

Mason has called me a great many nicknames but queen is a new one. "I've been upgraded from princess."

He laughs against my cheek. "I suppose you have."

My body aches with all I've been through but there is still a part of me that wants to be close to him, to feel him inside me.

But as I move to deepen the kiss, he eases away. "Tonight is about your recovery."

I let out a long sigh. "Really?"

"Really." He settles me into his body. "Besides, you're going to need your energy for moving."

"Moving?" I manage to push up at that declaration. "Move where?"

"Not sure," he answers, sinking down into the pillow under his head. "Somewhere the Italians can't find. What do you think about Colorado? There'd be good natural photography there."

"We talked about this, Mason. You're not running. That's my issue, not yours." I do sit up then, the twinge of pain is worth being able to twist around to really look at him.

"I'm not running," he answers, sliding his hand down my leg. "I'm still going to run the business, I'll just focus on asset management, leaving daily operations to my family. Roman can take over the casinos, Jake the construction, Luke can handle all the properties like these, and Leo..."

My brows lift as I look at him, wondering what he's thinking for Leo.

"I think he might be good at running the nightclubs."

That would be an excellent position for him. "You're going to forgive him then?"

"There was truth to your words about needing to trust Leo more. In fairness, I didn't trust myself either, but he's so like my father..." He sits up too, his forehead pressing to mine. "It's time to put the past in the past and move forward with a lot more love."

My eyes close and I can't help it, tears fill my eyes. "I think the same. I've let my own past, my worry that everyone who loves me will leave—"

"I am never leaving you." Mason lifts me into his lap. "I need you to understand, Charlotte. You are my future. You're stuck with me and even if you try to run, I'm a tough guy to shake."

"I'm not running," I whisper. "You're my family now, Mason."

"Charlotte, I'm going to ask now..."

I gasp. Somehow, I didn't quite picture my marriage proposal being in bed while wearing a sling and covered in bruises.

I had pictured champagne and candlelight. Then again, we had that when he bought the ring. And when has anything in our relationship been normal?

"Will you be my wife?"

"Yes." I don't need to think to answer. It's automatic. Mason and I belong together.

CHAPTER THIRTY-TWO

CHARLOTTE

MASON RETURNS to the bedroom with two champagne glasses, and I have to laugh. Wish and, when you're with Mason, you receive.

I didn't even say the words out loud, but somehow, he knew. He has candles in hand as well, and he lights them on the nightstand and dresser, turning off the lights as he hands me a glass.

"To us and our future," he says as we touch glasses, a satisfying tinkling sound tickling my ears.

I take a drink and then wrinkle my nose, looking down at my glass. "What is this?"

"Sparkling cider," he answers, sitting next to me on the bed.

"I am over twenty-one, you know."

He chuckles. "True. But you also took heavy-duty pain medication today and I need to make sure I'm taking good care of you."

My stomach drops because...yeah...it's been a long time since anyone worried about my health like this.

I want to sink into this feeling. Mason has done what no one has for such a long time.

Not only has he made me feel loved, he's taken my problems and one at a time, he's made them disappear. I haven't been this light in years.

I'd been drowning for so long. Mason wasn't just a raft or a lifeline, he was an island. More than that, he was paradise.

I was never leaving.

I take another sip of my sparkling cider and then I set down the glass. "We're getting married and we're celebrating with no alcohol and no sex."

Mason cocks a brow. "You are displeased, my queen?"

"I am."

He sets his glass down too as he scratches his chin. "I might have an idea."

And then he picks up two of the candles and carries them to the bathroom.

I'm still sitting there wondering what he's up to when he comes back out and gets the others. It's on the tip of my tongue to ask if he's planning to leave me in the dark when I hear the water start in the tub.

A sigh escapes my lips. Our last bath had been heaven and it's the perfect way to soothe my aching body and celebrate.

He comes out of the bathroom once again and gently helps me from the bed, stripping off my clothes, even the sling with the greatest tenderness and care.

The tub full, he helps me in.

I sit in the middle of the massive tub as I watch him undress too. He's got a few new cuts and bruises as well, compliments of Leo, I'm sure.

But even with the marks, he's steal-my-breath gorgeous and I try to process that this man is going to be mine.

All mine.

He reaches into his bathroom cabinet and pulls out several small bottles.

"Bubble bath?" I ask, my lips parting in pleasure.

He returns my smile. "Too drying. These are essential oils." And then he uncorks the first bottle and climbs into the tub behind me.

Settling onto his chest, he waves the first one under my nose. "Lavender."

"Very nice," I reply, the smell filling my nose.

He uncorks the next. "Rose."

My nose wrinkles. It's a bit strong.

"Frankincense."

"No." I shake my head. "I like the lavender."

"Lavender it is."

I expect him to add it to the water but instead, he pours some into his hand, and then begins rubbing my chest with his lubricated palms. His touch is light, easy, it goes over my bruised skin without a bother and down my arm, actually easing some of the ache.

He does the other side and then his hand dips under the water, rubbing across my belly. He just gets to my pelvis, my body beginning to vibrate with anticipation when he shifts and begins doing my back.

On and on it goes, his hands soothing the aches of my skin and heating me until I'm ready to start begging again when he finally massages my behind, and then slips his hand between my thighs, rubbing the oil over my seam.

It both soothes my flesh and makes me moan in pleasure.

Very gently, Mason wraps an arm about my injured one, holding it against my body the way my sling had done.

"We're going to go slow and careful," he whispers in my ear. "I can't have you hurt any more than you already do."

I've never felt safer or more protected than I do in this moment, the oil soothing my skin, his touch making me yearn for more.

I'm wrapped in his strong embrace as he slides his hand over my sex again, his touch so slow and gentle, I give a whimper of impatience.

He smiles against my neck and then removes his hand.

A cry of protest falls from my lips and his smile grows as he adds more oil to his fingertips.

And then he dips his hand back under the water, sliding his freshly oiled fingers over my lips.

I arch into his touch, even as he holds my torso steady. I want more of everything he's giving, but he keeps his movements slow and easy, the rhythm the sweetest torture until I'm ready to burst from my need.

And that's when he softly lifts my pelvis to slide his cock inside me.

The oil has made me slick enough that it doesn't hurt at all this time, in fact, he feels so good, I arch into him and tweak my arm the slightest bit.

At my mewl of pain, he goes rigid and still underneath me. "What hurt, love?"

"My arm. I just..."

He laces his fingers through mine, holding me against him as he works his hips, doing all the moving. I'm nearly immobile.

It's a feat of athleticism I might marvel at if I wasn't so busy feeling fantastic.

His cock presses on every point of pleasure inside me, the orgasm that's been building makes my thighs shake with need.

And then he slides his free hand back over my sex, his middle fingers pressing against my clit.

I can't hold it back as I cry out, exploding around him. But he's not done...

He keeps pistoning in and out of me, his fingers sliding over my clit until my breath is completely ragged again.

I wish I could wrap my arm behind me and around his neck but being cradled like this is a fabulous second option as he holds my entire body suspended against his.

He's making these grunts in my ear, his breathing rough as his heart thunders against my back and I know he's getting close too.

I'm going to cum again and it's a race to see which one of us will be first.

"Mason," I beg, calling his name. "Oh God. Mason," I'm gasping with pleasure, my eyes tightly squeezed shut.

He knows I'm close again and two more fingers press to my sensitive clit, making me orgasm for a second time as I scream his name.

That's all he can take, and he roars into my neck as he cums.

I wilt against him, the warm water, the oil, and the multiple orgasms sapping me of all my energy.

We sit there for a few minutes, slowly floating down, as he peppers kisses over my skin. Finally, he lifts me from the bath, wrapping me in a fluffy towel.

I turn to him, placing a soft kiss on the corner of his mouth. "I love you."

He pulls me close. "I love you too, sweetheart. Now and forever."

"Let's go to bed."

He puts the sling back on my arm before we settle into his bed, my body cocooned against his.

I sigh out my contentment knowing this is going to be how I sleep for the rest of my life.

How did I manage it? I fell in love with Mason and by some miracle of fate, he loves me back.

EPILOGUE

Kim

"It's almost disgusting," I mutter to myself as I look out the window at the picturesque mountains beyond.

The morning of Charlotte and Mason's wedding is a perfect Colorado spring day. It rained last night, I could hear it on the roof, but today, the world is bright and shiny for the washing it received the night before.

The grass is a brilliant green, the sky a bright blue dotted with white puffy clouds, the Aspen pines a perfect shade of dark green.

I stare out the window of the honeymoon suite I shared last night with my best friend Charlotte and marvel at the perfection. When you have money, even nature works to please you.

We're at some high-end hotel and resort in Aspen, the sort that I've never even dreamed of staying in. One night probably costs more than my whole month's rent. I don't know because Charlotte's fiancé Mason paid for my flight here and my room, along with all the extras.

Which is crazy to me, I'm not even using the room he paid for since I kept Charlotte company last night. I keep track of every penny, I have to, and waste is currently not in my vocabulary.

This room is twice the size of my apartment in Las Vegas, and I share that place with three other dancers.

It's a lavish display of wealth that makes my head spin.

But the money is not what deep down unsettles me. The Kincaids, all five of them, are what really make me nervous. They are all handsome as sin, with their dark hair and their piercing brown eyes. Each of them is as rich as he is successful.

But they all have this edge. You can feel it under the surface.

Dangerous.

They are as intoxicating as they are nerve-wracking, and I've been on edge since I got here. Especially when the second Kincaid brother enters the room, Leo Kincaid. He's more of everything.

More muscles, more good lucks, more sinister charm that sets my teeth on edge and my pulse fluttering. Which is a reaction I can ill afford. I'm so close to realizing my dreams, I cannot afford a distraction now, no matter how tempting.

I'd be more worried about Charlotte and what she's getting into, except Mason seems to worship her.

And by extension, he's lavished me with gifts. Plane ticket, room, dress, spa day.

I have exactly enough money to pay for myself to fly from here to New York tomorrow morning to attend my interview with the New York ballet company and not a penny more if I'm going to pay rent this month.

In fact, I'm pretty sure I'm going to have to sleep in the airport before my return flight the next day.

But I don't care about that. This interview is a dream come true and my one chance at having the career no one from my hometown would ever imagine. The one my mother dreamed of and never got the chance to have because she had me instead.

Charlotte is still asleep as I sit by the window, staring at the lush garden below, the staff already hard at work making the perfect garden even better for the upcoming ceremony.

The gazebo is decorated with a gauzy fabric that floats in the morning breeze while white chairs are set at perfect angles.

A little sigh escapes my lips. I might be cautious around the Kincaids, but I'm still a bit jealous about the way they live.

Still, I'm going to hold to the plan for a little while longer to make my dreams come true.

A soft knock sounds at the door, and I get up to answer it, tightening the lush robe around my waist, before I crack the door open.

Mason is standing on the other side. He's the picture of business casual masculine elegance this morning. With his pressed slacks and his white shirt, tucked in but open a single button at the collar.

I've never been into guys who are that perfectly coiffed, not a hair out of place, but I can't deny he cuts quite the figure.

Charlotte did well. Though, I always knew she would. Stunningly gorgeous, quiet and shy, she has this demure grace that makes men like Mason froth. Charlotte and I waited tables together at a Bar called Rebel's. The serious businessmen who came in always gave Charlotte a long look.

"Morning," I whisper.

"Good morning," he murmurs back. "Charlotte still asleep?"

I nod. "Yeah. I can wake her if you want."

"No," he shakes his head. "I just wanted to know how she slept."

Man oh man, this guy's got it bad. I duck my head to hide my smile, a different touch of envy settling in my chest. What would it be like to have someone care for me like this? It makes me ache deep down to think it.

But with my gaze cast down, I almost miss the fact that Leo has appeared until he's right next to Mason. I feel a blush climb my cheeks as our gazes connect.

If Mason is too coiffed, Leo is the exact brand of sexy that makes my brain fritz. He's got on a fitted T-shirt and tight jeans, the kind that show off his many, many muscles.

Bulkier, rougher than his brother, he looks like trouble in the best way possible. Not that I'm looking for problems, but if I were...

My gaze snaps back to Mason, who is scowling at Leo. Charlotte mentioned tension between the two brothers, and I feel it now.

Clearing my throat, I give Mason a bright smile. "We went to bed early, promise." I draw an X over my heart.

His gaze returns to me, softening. "Thanks, Kim. Don't forget to go to the desk and get a key for your room tonight. I've also arranged for a car to take you to the airport tomorrow morning. If there is anything else you need, don't hesitate to ask."

I nod as I look the other way, not meeting the eye of either Kincaid brother. "Thank you, Mason. I really appreciate it." My dad was never around, I was raised by my mom, and she worked three jobs just to keep a roof over our heads and food on the table.

"Not a problem at all."

I swallow down a lump. I won't ask him for hotel money for New York, I know he means if I need anything for this wedding, but I briefly wonder if I should give dating another try.

I've had one boyfriend in my entire life, and it was an underwhelming and somewhat humiliating experience. But it would be nice to have someone look out for me now and then. "I'm really happy for you and Charlotte."

Leo has been silent next to his brother, his dark brown eyes assessing me. My skin goosepimples as I turn to meet his gaze again.

Did I call the Kincaids dangerous? Leo's eyes alone are downright lethal, and my gaze drops as I nip at my lip. I've never had a reaction like this to a man and I'm not quite sure what to do with it.

"Morning, gorgeous," he says with a one-sided grin that makes my stomach do somersaults.

He's got this stubble that's not quite a shadow but it's not a beard either, and it only highlights the fullness of his mouth and the square jaw that makes him look all man. His hair is a bit mussed, but somehow, it only adds to his appeal, like he just got out of bed…

I clear my throat. "Good morning."

Mason scowls at Leo. "Your dress should be delivered in the next half hour. I took the liberty of choosing a pale green that should complement your hair and eyes."

I don't even ask how he might have gotten the size correct. Something tells me it will fit perfectly. "I'm sure it's lovely. Thank you again, Mason."

Leo's smile grows and I shift in the doorway.

"Mason? Is that you?" I hear Charlotte call from behind me.

I look back to see her rising from the bed. "You're not supposed to see him," I say, closing the door a little tighter around my body to block the view.

"I won't," Charlotte says as she wraps a robe about her body, the same white hotel one I'm wearing. The difference is she has a high-end negligee under hers and I've got a ratty T-shirt under mine. "I just want to talk to him through a crack in the door."

I've no choice but to step out into the hall, my bare feet on full display. At least Mason had sent a manicurist to do our fingers and toes last night. Mine have a fresh coat of pale pink polish on them that should go nicely with the dress. I curl them into the carpet as Leo gives me a long look up and down, the sort that makes my skin heat. "I don't know if you remember, but we've met before."

I shake my head. I don't really, and I feel like I would. He's not the kind of man a girl forgets.

I know the story. Charlotte went on a couple of dates with Leo a few years back and that's how she met Mason.

Leo came into the bar on a night we were both working. Case in point, he asked Charlotte out that night and not me. I don't make an impression on rich and successful guys. Not like she does.

Then again, I was probably hustling like nobody's business the night he came in.

I have a full scholarship to UNLV so I don't have to pay tuition, but the rest of my life, including all the costs of training as a dancer, I've had to finance on my own and tips is the way I make it happen most nights.

My mom has nothing to spare to help me.

"Sort of…" I say as I look down the hall. Anywhere but at him.

"I remember you."

He steps closer and I can feel the heat of him, my nipples actually stiffen as I wrap the robe tighter around me again.

What would it be like to have a man like this in my bed? My body pulses with a delicious ache at the idea of it, a feeling I try to tamp down.

I have a confession to make. I've only ever slept with one guy and he never actually made me…

I swallow down a lump. "You do?"

Next to me, Mason is whispering to Charlotte through the crack in the door, his hand pressed to the thick wood as though he'd like to bust down the door, but I can't make out a word he's saying. My whole body is focused on Leo.

I close my eyes, my chin titling up and to the side. Why I'm exposing my neck to a man I just called lethal, I don't know…

"I do." His hand comes to the wall behind me, the one I just realized I'm leaning against, his thumb brushing the indent of my waist. "And I have to confess, I'm disappointed you don't remember me."

There is no point in lying. Tomorrow I'll leave and then I'll likely never see Leo again. "I seriously doubt I'll forget you after today."

I feel him grin. Don't even ask me how that's possible but I do as he shifts closer. "Oh yeah… why is that?"

"You're…" I search for the right word. Hot as Hades? Tall, dark, and sinister? "Magnetic."

His hand slides down the wall, his thumb tracing my hip. "Right back at you."

"Hello," a female voice calls from the other end of the hall. My eyes snap open. Mason and Leo's sister, Arabella, is walking toward us with an army of people behind her. "The cavalry has arrived!"

A rack of dresses is at the back of the group, along with several women carrying cases of different shapes and sizes.

We're all about to get major makeovers. Again.

This is Charlotte's life now? It's not without its appeal.

Leo pushes back and regret lances through me as I stand up straight, pasting a smile on my face.

An hour later, my long red hair has been twisted into some amazingly elaborate coif at the back. The dress is the perfect shade to highlight my green eyes, only further accentuated by the subtle shades of eyeliner and shadow.

And the mermaid style dress hugs my dancer's body like it was custom made for me though I never gave anyone a single measurement.

And Charlotte...

She's never looked more beautiful. Draped in white, the strapless princess gown shows off her lusher curves and classic beauty.

Her hair is down, one section pulled back with a comb at her right ear, and styled in lose waves that only make her cheekbones look even more classic and her large gray eyes even wider.

I sigh next to Arabella, Charlotte's other bridesmaid.

Charlotte is perfection.

A spread of food has been laid out in the room as we wait for the ceremony to begin, but I only pick at it. I'm nervous, which is odd. I don't mind being in front of people, it's part of being on stage, so I try to determine why I'm feeling so off.

And then I remember. Leo Kincaid. He's going to see me in this dress. And for once I look like I actually belong in their world.

Maybe I can pretend for one night...

Leo seemed interested.

And I'd love to know what all the fuss was about. And by fuss, I mean sex. Charlotte is discreet, she hasn't said much, but what she has shared tells me that the bedroom is steaming hot between her and Mason.

Making our way outside, we're not waiting for more than a minute before the delicate strains of a melodious violin announce it's time for us to walk down the aisle.

Grace is kind of my thing, but my gaze catches Leo's as he waits at the other end of the aisle with his brother. His gaze locks on mine and I nearly trip.

It takes all my concentration to focus on Mason and Charlotte as they say their vows, promise to love, honor, and cherish each other for the rest of their lives.

I can hear the happiness in Charlotte's voice, the promise in Mason's just before they seal their bond with a kiss.

It's so beautiful, I forget about the danger a man like Leo would bring into my life. He's a predator and I'm no match. But I don't care about that or my carefully crafted reasons for not having meaningless trysts. And after a glass of champagne, every reservation I had has disappeared as I step out onto the veranda to watch the sun set behind the mountains.

It was a perfect day. One I'd like to remember when I'm back in Vegas hustling drinks at Rebel's.

Or maybe, I'll be in New York preparing to be a professional dancer…

With a sigh, I look back and that's when I find Leo standing in the doorway behind me. My pulse stutters as a blush fills my cheeks. "Hello."

"The bride and groom are about to retire for the evening."

"Already?" I ask, and then my cheeks heat even more. Like I needed to ask why.

"My brother is very enamored with his bride."

I nod, determined not to make this anymore awkward. But Leo does that for me, moving so close I can feel my nipples tighten again.

Only this dress didn't really allow for a bra, the spaghetti straps and draped neckline making sure my small bit of cleavage is on full display.

Leo looks down and I see his eyes darken. He's noticed my nipples too.

"You know…" he leans close to my ear. "I've got a beautiful view of the rising moon from my room and tonight, it's full."

My pulse rushes in my ears as I nip at my lip. Do I actually dare to do this? Wetting my lips, I force myself to look over my shoulder and meet his gaze. He's even more handsome in his tux than he was in his T-shirt this morning.

What's more, the promise I see in his eyes has me gasping for breath.

Yeah. I think I dare…

KEEP READING to get another epilogue from Mason!

But also… get ready for Leo to heat up the page! Order today!

King of Temptation!

BONUS EPILOGUE

Bonus Epilogue
Mason

It's got to be two in the morning as Charlotte curls into me, her breath still heavy from her lastest orgasm.

We'd fallen asleep but I'd woken her again two hours later because marrying her today has not diminished my appetite, in fact, I'm bordering on insatiable.

I'm never getting enough of this woman.

She winds an arm over her shoulder, threading her fingers into my hair. Her shoulder has healed nicely over the last six weeks, no surgery required. "Everything was perfect today."

It was. Almost.

Charlotte looked as beautiful as I'd ever imagined. I look over the side of the bed at the crumpled gown on the floor. I'd had fun fucking her from behind with the layers of skirts billowing around us.

Aspen was stunning with its natural beauty and the fresh scent of pine. Our new home is a few hours east of here. We'll stay until Vegas has been managed and then we'll move back and forth between whatever home I buy in Vegas and the ranch.

And for our wedding, the hotel had gone above and beyond with service, food, and décor.

The one black spot on the day…fucking Leo. Since Charlotte had healed so nicely, I'd been forgiving and invited him to attend our wedding, even allowing him to stand with the family at the altar.

But as usual, Leo was causing trouble. He'd been making eyes at Charlotte's best friend all day.

Kim was a beauty. There was no denying it. Tall, willowy, and graceful, with bright red hair and light green eyes, she was striking. I could see why Leo was interested, but Charlotte's best friend was off limits. A fact I'd explain very soon.

"What is perfect, is being back in bed with you. I hated last night."

"Your brothers didn't keep you company?"

"I see them all the time." I slide my hand down her bare belly. "I don't have much chance to miss them like you have Kim. Did the two of you have fun?"

Charlotte smiles over her shoulder. "It was wonderful to see her, but I missed you last night too."

And then she gives me one of those kisses that I love, all soft and sweet.

"I'm sorry she has to fly out so early tomorrow. It's not very restful."

My fingers dip between Charlotte's legs as I lick behind her ear, sucking on that spot where I can feel her thrumming pulse. "I hired her a car to make it easier."

"Thank you, Mason. Kim and I only had each other when we didn't have anyone else, and I really appreciate you taking care of her."

I straighten up, my fingers stilling. "I'm worried about the way Leo was eyeing her."

But Charlotte shakes her head. "Don't. Kim doesn't date, like ever."

"You didn't either. Until you did." And then my fingers dive back in. Because I married the love of my life and I'm going to enjoy it.

But I make a mental note. Keep tabs on my brother. He's still on my shit list and I won't have any problem giving him a beating if he needs one.

And I'll keep an eye on Kim too.

Because if she's important to Charlotte, then she's important to me.

But that can wait until morning. Right now, I'm going make love to my wife. Again...

Hey! Thank you so much for reading! This is the first book in a new contemporary line of Dark, steamy billionaire romances with some real mafia vibes! But trust me when I tell you that my historical have all the same feels! My dukes and earls are alphas with attitude and they don't mind bending the rules to get what they desire...

Want to check out a few? Here are some fan favorites!

A Bargain with a Beast - Her new employer might be the most beastly man she's ever met, until she sees him holding his daughter....what would it be like to be protected by arms like that?

A Masquerade With a Marquess - She might be blind but even she can SEE that the man she's been forced to marry is trouble.

A Vengeful Viscount - It wasn't until the doctor's told her she was dying that she decided she wanted to really live. The dark and delicious Viscount hunting her horrid fiancé.... He's the perfect man to help her.

MARQUESS OF
Fortune
TAMMY
ANDRESEN
BEST
SELLER
A DATE WITH A
Duke
Marquess

STALK ME LIKE AN ALPHA!

Join my newsletter to get all the latest updates!

Tammy's Newsletter

And follow me everywhere else for teasers, giveaway, book news and fun!

www.authortammyandresen.com
www.facebook.com/authortammyandresen
www.instagram.com/tammyandresen
https://www.tiktok.com/@lordsoflasvegas
www://amazon.com/authortammyandresen

MORE ABOUT TAMMY

Tammy is the writer of Bestselling Regency Romance who could not resist the urge of writing in the dark and delicious world of Contemporary Dark and Steamy Billionaire Romance.

She lives with her husband and three children in Massachusetts and her favorite adventures are the ones that are found in books but occasionally she lives a few of her own!

Made in the USA
Las Vegas, NV
15 May 2026

47037727R00132